Rebel Without A Clue

Second Edition

Rebel Without A Clue

Second Edition

Mike Faricy

Library of Congress Control Number: 2023918915
paperback ISBN: 978-1-962080-59-0
e-Book ISBN: 978-1-962080-60-6

MJF Publishing books may be purchased for education, Business, or promotional use. For information on bulk purchases, please contact the author directly at mikefaricyauthor@gmail.com

Published by

MJF Publishing
https://www.mikefaricybooks.com

Acknowledgments

I would like to thank the following people for their help and support:

Special thanks to my editors, Kitty, Donna and Rhonda for their hard work, cheerful patience and positive feedback.

I would like to thank Ann and Julie for their creative talent and not slitting their wrists or jumping off the high bridge when dealing with my Neanderthal computer capabilities.

Special thanks to Ann for her patience.

Last, I would like to thank family and friends for their encouragement and unqualified support. Special thanks to Maggie, Jed, Schatz, Pat, Av, Emily and Pat for not rolling their eyes, at least when I was there, and most of all, to my wife Teresa whose belief, support and inspiration has from day one, never waned.

Prologue

Morton and I stopped for just one in The Spot at the end of our walk. Since Morton couldn't see above the bar, he did his usual straining against the leash and almost tore my right arm from the socket as he charged along the bar toward Louie's stool. He rounded the corner of the bar, came to a screeching halt, and stared at Louie's empty bar stool. He quickly glanced around and then gave a whine when he couldn't see Louie anywhere.

"Get you a beer?" Mike, the bartender, asked as he grabbed a clean mug from the back of the bar.

"Yeah, thanks, the usual IPA, Mike."

"Louie still working?" he asked, sounding surprised.

"No, he's got a bit of a head cold, so he's at home in recovery." Louie was home convinced he had contracted Covid. I was pretty sure he had just picked up a head cold. The result of spending last night passed out in his car across the street from the office. I didn't want to mention Covid for fear Mike would make me drink my beer outside.

"Here you go, Dev," he said as he slid the beer mug across the bar. "Put it on your tab?"

"No, surprisingly, I've actually got some cash. Better give me a bag of pork rinds, too, while I'm thinking of it."

At the sound of the words 'pork rinds,' Morton's tail began to wag and slap against the side of the bar. I opened the bag, poured half into my hand, and bent down to Morton. He inhaled the things in about a half second. Not one of them fell to the floor. I settled onto Louie's stool, glanced around the bar at the dozen or so people, and took a sip of beer.

I was halfway through my beer when the front door opened. In stepped a woman with long dark hair and a beautiful figure. She was clad in very tight jeans and a gray tank top with half the buttons undone, revealing a very enticing cleavage. She took a couple of steps, scanned the crowd, and then headed down the bar. The conversation level definitely lowered as heads turned to watch. Some woman in a booth punched the guy she was with on the shoulder to get his attention back.

I figured the dark-haired beauty was meeting up with one of the three guys in the softball uniforms who had come in a few minutes earlier, but she sauntered right past them, causing all three heads to turn and follow her as she came around the corner, struck a pose, and said, "Hi, you wouldn't happen to be Dev Haskell, would you?"

She didn't appear to be serving a court document or an arrest warrant, so I said, "Yeah, I am, and you are?"

Morton was on his feet and immediately shoved his nose between her legs. "Oh, how cute," she said. "My name is Tracey Wilde. I got your name from a friend. You investigate stuff, don't you?"

"Yeah, I'm a private investigator. Morton sit," I said, and surprisingly, he did. "Are you thinking you might need help with something?"

Her dark blue eyes flashed, and she said, "Not exactly. It's kind of a long story. I've just separated from my husband, and I'm thinking about maybe filing for divorce. Do you do that kind of thing, investigate husbands?"

"Well, if you're filing for a divorce—"

"I'm just thinking about it. I haven't done it yet. That's why I want someone to check him out. He started his own business, and he works all sorts of crazy hours. At least that's what he's telling me, but I think he might not be telling me the truth."

"So you think he's having an affair with someone?"

"Maybe. I just don't know. That's what I want to find out."

"Has he been abusive to you?"

"No, well, at least not yet."

"Are you worried he might be abusive?"

"I just want to be careful. I told him I didn't want to live with him anymore, told him he had to move out."

"And did he?" I asked. My first thought was that telling her husband he had to move out seemed like a pretty strong response to someone working long hours in a new business.

She seemed to think about that for a moment, then nodded and said, "Yeah, he moved a couple of months ago. I had to tell him a number of times, but he eventually got the message. I sold the place as soon as he was out."

"Okay, I think it might be best if we met at my office or a place of your choice if you'd feel more comfortable somewhere else."

She smiled and said, "I guess your office would be okay. Should I call your secretary and make an appointment?"

Since I didn't have a secretary and my calendar was completely open, I pulled my wallet out and handed her my business card. "Call any time, and I'll adjust whatever is scheduled so we can meet."

"How about if I just show up at 10:00 tomorrow morning?"

"Sure, I'll move some things around, and that should work. Maybe call before you come just to be sure I'm in the office. I'm working on a couple of big cases, and it's possible something might come up, but I should probably be there."

She glanced at my business card and said, "Mmm-mmm, I like this. Okay, sorry to interrupt your evening." She glanced over at the four empty stools between the other single guy in the place and me. A half-finished beer was on the bar in front of him. He'd been too busy studying her figure to have touched the beer recently.

"Not a problem, you're really not interrupting. I just stopped to talk to the bartender. I'm looking into something for him," I lied.

"Oh, cool," she said and held out her hand. I extended my hand to shake hers. She immediately wrapped both soft, warm hands around my hand. She smiled, raised her eyebrows, and rubbed her thumbs on the palm and the back of my hand as she said, "Thank you. I look forward to getting to know you a lot better. Have a nice evening. I'll be thinking of you, and I'll see you in the morning." She waited a moment before she stepped back, blew me a kiss, and headed toward the front door. Multiple heads turned as she walked past. As soon as she stepped out the door, one of the guys at the end of the bar called my name and gave me a thumbs-up.

"Was that the latest hot number you're seeing?" Mike asked as he stepped in front of me.

"No, just a new client. She's like all my clients. She's just excited to be involved with me."

"Well, if she ever comes in again, I'll have to set her straight. You ready for another beer?"

"I'd love one, but I'm gonna take a pass and head home."

"They'll all think you're going after that sexy chick."

"You can tell them she begged me to stop over, and I didn't want to disappoint her."

One

The following morning, I was up almost an hour before my alarm went off. Three different times over the course of the night, I woke up to check the time and then went right back to sleep. There was no way I was going to get back to sleep now, so I shaved, showered, and put on clean jeans and a pressed shirt in anticipation of my 10:00 appointment with the lovely Tracey Wilde. I checked the clock, only five hours to go. I looked her up on Facebook and Instagram. I couldn't find her on LinkedIn. Her Facebook page had a number of pictures of her. In fact, that was about all there was on her site. Pictures of her in formal dresses, pictures with a number of different men I presumed to be friends. Pictures of her working out in a bikini and drinking champagne in bed. There were a half-dozen shots of her walking on an ocean beach. A bunch of pictures of her sitting around a swimming pool and three images where she was leaning against an expensive-looking blue coupe. All the images appeared to be professionally taken, and I wondered if she might be a fashion model.

Her Facebook site didn't have any personal information listing a job or where she was from. There was nothing indicating she was married or in a relationship. I'd get the lowdown on all that during our 10:00 meeting. As soon as Morton finished his morning task and ate his breakfast, we hurried down to the office. Louie wasn't in, but that wasn't really a surprise. I wished him a speedy recovery but hoped he didn't make an appearance until my meeting with Tracey was finished. I had ninety minutes before the meeting, when I started to clean the office.

I put on a fresh pot of coffee, emptied the wastebaskets, recycled the beer cans along with an empty bourbon bottle, and rinsed out both coffee mugs. I borrowed the vacuum from the hairdressers across the way and vacuumed the place probably for the first time in close to three years. I used paper towels to dust the tops of the file cabinets. I tossed a pair of insulated overalls, two fishing poles, a tackle box, and a softball jersey into the back closet. I placed a stack of old files on my desk and set Louie's yellow legal pad next to the stack of files so that it looked like I was involved in a number of cases. I began staring out the window at 9:45. Fifty minutes later, I'd pretty much given up and had just decided Tracey wasn't going to make an appearance when my cell phone rang.

"Haskell Investigations, how can I help y'all?" I answered, faking a Southern accent and crossing my fingers.

"I'd like to speak with Dev Haskell, please," a voice that sounded like Tracey said.

"One moment, please," I replied, then pressed one of the keys on my laptop to make a bell sound before I said, "Dev Haskell."

"Oh, hi, Dev. Glad I got you. This is Tracey. Sorry I'm calling so late. In fact, I'm just pulling up in front of your office. I forgot I had a massage scheduled this morning."

"Not a problem. Come on up. I'll have a coffee ready for you."

I glanced out the window just as a dark-blue two-door coupe pulled to the curb behind my 2012 Dodge Charger. I'd bought my car at the police auction two years ago for seven grand. I pulled the binoculars from my desk drawer and scanned the coupe just as the driver's door opened, and beautiful, sexy Tracey stepped out. She was wearing heels, a short black leather skirt, and a white blouse that revealed a good deal of her wonderful cleavage. She carried what looked like a white bakery box. I quickly rolled my desk chair back as she waited for a guy in a pickup to pass.

He slowed, honked, gave her a wave, and headed up the street. She crossed the street and stepped into the building. A moment later, I heard a slight creak on the staircase as she made her way up to the second floor.

There was a soft knock on the door as it opened, and Tracey stepped in. If she was surprised by the look of the place with Louie's picnic table desk, my scratched antique wooden desk with mismatched client chairs, or Morton's ragged pillow that he'd just jumped off of, she didn't let on.

"Hi, Dev. Hope I didn't screw up your morning," she said as Morton inserted his nose beneath her short black leather skirt. She smiled at him, scratched his head, and handed me the bakery box. "I thought I'd better bring a little treat since I know you're really busy, and I'm really late."

"It's not a problem. I had more than enough to do," I said as I nodded toward the stack of files and Louie's legal pad. I set the bakery box on my desk, opened it up, and stared at four delicious muffins.

"I hope you like blueberry muffins."

"I love them. How did you know? Grab a seat and let me pour you a coffee. Do you take it black?"

"Mmm-mmm, if you have a little cream and sugar, I'd love it."

"Not a problem," I said and opened the top file drawer. I'd borrowed a bowl of plastic cream containers and sugar packets from a restaurant last year, and since Louie and I took our coffee black, the bowl was still full. I set the bowl in front of Tracey, filled Louie's mug for her, and set it on the desk. I filled my mug and settled into my desk chair.

Tracey seemed to be searching for something in her black leather purse. I was just about to ask what she was looking for when she smiled and said, "Oh, finally, here you go," she said to Morton and held out a large dog biscuit. Morton snatched it from her hand and hurried back to his pillow.

"Oh, man, he'll probably want to go home with you. Thank you, that was very nice."

"I think he's just a sweetie."

"Give it some time," I said. "So, you said last night you wanted me to take a look at your husband. Let's start with a little background information. Do you mind if I take some notes?" I flipped the page on Louie's legal pad and wrote Tracey's name at the top.

"No, I guess that's okay. Well, let's see. I grew up on the East side. Went to high school at Johnson. Took a couple of semesters at the U and didn't like it at all. I got into modeling, and that's worked out very well."

"You still involved in modeling?"

"Yes, but when I first started, I was taking any job offer I could get. After a couple of years, I landed a position with an agency. That led to some film work and industry work. After a year of that, I started my own agency, representing myself, and I've been doing that ever since."

"So, you're self-employed?"

"Yes, through the agency I run."

I made a two-word note on the legal pad, 'Agency/Self.' "What was your maiden name?"

"Oh, I never changed it. I kept my own last name. I told my soon-to-be ex-husband that I didn't want to change my name, and he said I could call myself Little

Red Riding Hood for all he cared, just as long as I married him."

"That sounds nice."

"Yeah, he's a nice guy, or at least he was, but we've both changed. I guess that happens. Anyway, I kept my name. My full name is Tracey Desiree Wilde. My last name ends with an 'e.'"

"And could you spell your middle name for me?"

She did and then added, "I thought long and hard about dropping the second 'e' at the end, but then decided I'd be dealing with misspellings for the rest of my life, so I just let it go."

"And how long have you been married?"

"It's been almost three years."

"What's your husband's name?"

She smiled and said, "Percy Riggs. His middle name is Eugene." She spelled his name out for me.

"You said he moved out. Where did he move to?"

"He's still in town. He lives on the third floor of a house on Lincoln Ave. Maybe a mile or so from the Cathedral. I don't know the address. Do you know that area?"

I nodded and said, "Yeah, I'm from the city, and I live four or five blocks up the street from the Cathedral, so I'm familiar with the area."

"You live in an old house?"

I nodded. "Yeah, it's coming up on a hundred and fifty years old. Speaking of which, I've got your phone number, but give me your address and your email address." I wrote them down and asked, "This is the house you and Percy lived in?"

"No."

"You own this home?"

"Yes, I moved a month or two ago. I've been so busy it feels like forever."

"How does Percy feel about you two?"

She shook her head. "He thinks that, given enough time, I'll want to get back together. I understand him thinking that, but it's getting to the point that the last thing I want to do is have him move back in, and we'll have to go through this all over again. Do you know what I mean?"

Having been dumped by uncountable women, I understood exactly what she was saying. "It's never any fun. So, tell me, what does he do? You said he started his own company."

She nodded, drank some coffee, and said, "He's always been a tech person. He's got a master's in computers, or the internet, or something like that. I'm not sure what it is. He's always worked in the computer world and has done pretty well. He started his own company not quite a year ago."

"What's the name of it?"

"His company? He named it after himself, Technical Percy."

"Technical Percy, that's the name of his company?"

"Yeah, and I get what you're probably thinking, but that's what he named it."

"And you told me that he's working a lot of hours."

"An unbelievable amount of hours. Seven days a week, fourteen or sixteen hours a day. He'd come home and go to bed. No interest in me. I mean, a couple of nights, I dressed in a negligee and waited for him to come home. He just looked at me and said he was too tired and that he'd catch me in the morning. The next morning when I woke up, he had already gone to his office."

We chatted back and forth for another hour. We each had a blueberry muffin, and I told Tracey I would check out her husband. No one was more surprised than me when she counted out ten one-hundred-dollar bills on my desk and said, "Let me know when you need more."

She gave me a lingering kiss on the cheek, said goodbye to Morton, and strutted out of the office. I watched her out the window as she climbed into her blue two-door coupe. I grabbed my binoculars, repeated the license plate number to myself until I'd written it down, and watched as she disappeared up the street.

TWO

I turned on my computer and Googled Technical Percy. The site popped up with a photo of Percy Riggs seated at a circular desk in shirt sleeves. He appeared to be in shape, not necessarily muscle-bound, but certainly not a lard ass. He was a nice-looking guy, smiling at the camera, and my first thought was, *If I was looking for a tech guy, I'd maybe contact him.* He was surrounded by three large computer monitors with all sorts of what looked like complex information on the screens. Along with a phone number, there was an address over in the Midway Industrial District. I wrote down the address and headed out to the car with Morton.

The Midway area was home to a number of small factories back in the 1920s and 30s. University Avenue ran more or less through the middle of the area. Obviously, things had changed over the course of the last century, and many of the four and five-story factory buildings that weren't torn down had been converted to condos or office buildings. Some structures had been torn down over the past thirty years and replaced by apartment buildings.

Technical Percy was located on North Hampden Ave. Not what you'd call a charming neighborhood, although there was nothing wrong with the area. It was just all older industrial structures. The address was a windowless, four-story brick building that had been painted a tan color. There was an entrance door in the center of the building and a mostly empty parking lot in front of the building. I pulled into the parking lot and parked next to a green Jeep Liberty with a rusted passenger door. A quick glance around didn't reveal any cars that gave the impression of fancy, which got me thinking of the two-door blue coupe that Tracey was driving.

Inside, a small lobby featured an elevator and a glass-enclosed sign listing the various businesses. Technical Percy was up on the fourth floor in unit 412. I pushed the button for the elevator and waited, then waited some more. I pushed the button three more times over the course of the next few minutes and finally decided that the staircase might be the better option. The factory, or whatever had been here before, had been divided up into small offices and theoretically updated. Clearly nothing had changed on the staircase since the original construction.

I made it up to the fourth floor and walked down the hallway. The offices all had wooden doors, so it was impossible to see inside. I walked past the Technical Percy office and down to the end of the hall counting twenty-four office doors. Only five were labeled with company names, one of which was Technical Percy. I walked back to the office, knocked as I opened the door, and stepped inside.

If the building hallway and the staircase appeared to be pretty low rent, Technical Percy looked like it came from a different universe. There were desks, electric cords, and computer screens everywhere in the large room. I made a mental note that there were no windows in the room. Three people, one of whom was Percy, were seated at desks, typing away on keyboards.

He looked just like his online photo. Fit and in shape, although you'd never describe him as muscular. He focused in on me staring wide-eyed at all the technology, and said, "Hi, can I help you?"

"I think I'm in the wrong place. I was looking for a friend of mine, Kevin O'Brien," I lied. "He doesn't happen to work here, does he?"

"No, I'm sorry, there's no one here by that name. What company does he work for? I can look it up and tell you where they are."

"Oh, thanks, but I don't know the name of the company. He just gave me the unit number, and I was sure he said 412."

"Sorry, wish I could help."

"Yeah, me too. What do you guys do, anyways?"

"Some aspects of tech."

"You lost me right there," I said. "Sorry to interrupt. Have a nice day."

"You do the same, sir. Hope you find your friend."

"I'll just give him a phone call. Thanks again," I said and stepped back into the hall.

My first impression was that Percy Riggs appeared to be a nice guy. I took the stairs down to the ground floor and headed out to the parking lot. Morton was half-asleep in the backseat. He raised an eyelid as I opened the driver's door, saw it was me, and went back to sleep. So much for security.

I pulled my phone out and called my pal, Dave McGovern, in the Department of Motor Vehicles. He'd been arrested for driving under the influence two years ago, and I'd put him in touch with Louie, who was able to get the charges dropped on a technicality. Dave was able to keep his job and said he owed me a favor for the rest of his life.

"McGovern," was how he answered my call.

"Hi Dave, Dev Haskell calling. Just checking in. How are things?"

"You know, Dev. Same day, different shit. Let me guess. You need some information on a license plate."

"Not exactly. I'm looking for the license number on a vehicle owned by a gentleman named Percy Riggs." I spelled the name for McGovern and added, "He's a St. Paul resident. I believe he lives on Lincoln Ave."

I could hear McGovern's fingers on his keyboard. A moment later, he said, "Yeah, this must be him, unit two at 716 Lincoln Avenue. Does that sound right?"

"Yeah, Dave, that sounds right. You have a license number on his car?"

"He's driving a white Chevy Equinox, a 2018. You got a color crayon and a clean spot on the wall?"

"Yeah, go ahead." I wrote the license plate number on my hand, told Dave thanks, and looked around the lot. There was a white car four spots off to the left. I backed out of my place and pulled alongside. Sure enough, it was a Chevy Equinox, and the license plate matched the number Dave McGovern had given me. I gave a quick look around, didn't see anyone, and climbed out. I walked around the vehicle, looking in the windows. There was nothing to see other than a long-handled brush to knock snow off the car.

I climbed back in my car and drove over to Lincoln Avenue. 716 was a three-story brick structure. I guessed the place was at least a hundred years old. There was a door off to the side that looked like an enclosed entrance that led up to the third floor. I went around the block and turned into the alley. The backyard housed a three-stall garage, an oak tree, and was fenced in by a six-foot wooden fence. All in all, it was a nice-looking place.

I drove back down to the office and pulled in behind Louie's faded Ford Fiesta. Morton and I hurried up the stairs to see Louie. He was seated at his picnic table desk, eating a blueberry muffin. His legal pad was in front of him.

"Hey, how are you feeling? It's great to see you."

"None the worse for wear. I tested negative for Covid the last two days and again this morning, so I finally decided to come into work."

"I can hear you're still plugged up."

"Yeah, I'm thinking I might give The Spot a pass tonight and head over to the gym and grab a sauna."

"You belong to a gym?"

He nodded and said, "Yeah, not that I ever use it."

"It's just good to see you back."

"Well, there's only so much time I can take watching the damn TV before I start to lose what's left of my mind. You look like you've been busy with all the files. New client?"

"Yes and no. Yeah, I've got a new client. A woman has me looking into her soon-to-be former husband. Just a quick glance today, and he seems like a pretty average guy. He started a tech business and is apparently working his ass off. She was in here this morning, and I stacked up those files and stole your legal pad just to make me look busy."

"But she hired you, right?"

"Yeah, and paid me in advance, in cash. So I'm not complaining. You got a court appearance later today?"

"No, fortunately. Things have been a little slow the last week or so, which turned out to be just fine. I'm in court tomorrow, and I have to get some things lined up. Hopefully, I'll be free of this cold by then. God, I'll tell you, I've been behaving at home the last couple of nights, and it's not fun."

"Well, maybe cut back on the times you spend sleeping in the car."

"Yeah, it's just that, at the time, that was the better choice than trying to drive home."

We spent the rest of the afternoon working. Louie had six or seven sneezing jags that went on for a dozen or more sneezes. Each time, I envisioned a cloud of cold germs heading my way. When he wasn't coughing and sneezing, I was searching the internet for information on Percy Riggs. There wasn't much other than he apparently had quite the reputation as a tech guy. He was involved in helping students in a local high school. He served on the board of directors for his church and volunteered to deliver Meals on Wheels.

Just before 5:00, Louie shut down his computer and stood up from his desk.

"You going to grab a sauna?" I asked.

"Well, I was thinking maybe it would be okay to head over to The Spot for just one. Care to join me?"

"We'll meet you over there," I said.

Three

Morton and I took our usual three-block walk. He got up close and personal with two fire hydrants and a tree. Along the way, we were passed by a black SUV. The first time, I really didn't pay any attention. The second time it passed, I figured it was maybe someone who didn't know the neighborhood. The third time I saw it, the car didn't pass us. Instead, it was parked a block away from The Spot and appeared to be watching Morton and me as we entered.

Once we stepped into The Spot, instead of heading down the bar to Louie, I stood by the small window with the red neon 'OPEN' sign and watched. A minute later, the SUV drove past. The same bald guy I'd seen previously was behind the wheel as the car headed up the street.

"Everything all right, Dev?"

"What? Oh yeah, Mike. Everything's fine. Hey, I'll have a beer and better give Louie a refill."

"Coming right up," he said as Morton pulled me down the length of the bar and around the corner to

Louie. When Morton turned the corner, Louie reached down with his handful of pork rinds.

"I gotta tell you, Louie. You were really missed by your biggest fan. I tried to take your place, but he wasn't all that thrilled."

"Who can blame him?" Louie said just as Mike delivered my beer and set a fresh drink in front of Louie.

"It's great to finally be back," Louie said and raised his glass. He drained what was left in the glass, placed it off to the side, and slid the fresh drink in front of him. Apparently, his idea of 'Just having one' was off the table. "Hey, congratulations on the new client. I know things have been a little slow for you the last couple of months."

"Hopefully, this is a sign they'll be picking up. You've been busy, haven't you?"

Louie nodded. "Yeah, up until a few days ago, but sooner or later, things will pick up, and then I'll be complaining about that."

"Feast or famine," I said. We chatted for another twenty minutes and finished our drinks. Louie served Morton the rest of the pork rinds and turned down my offer for another drink. We said good night to Mike and walked out to our cars.

Louie had always been the type of driver you preferred to have at least a block ahead of you. Tonight was no different. I watched him as he drove up the street and eventually turned at the stoplight. I glanced around for the black SUV, but thankfully, I didn't see it. I lost count of the number of times I checked my rearview mirror on the way home. I pulled into the driveway and parked in the garage for a change. No sign of the SUV as we headed for the back door. I ate cold pizza for dinner while standing at the kitchen counter and then settled in front of the TV. Apparently, whatever I was watching didn't quite keep my interest because I woke up just as the 10:00 news was ending.

Morton was already upstairs and stretched out on the bed. I set the alarm and was back asleep in a couple of minutes. I woke ten minutes before the alarm went off. I was dressed and downstairs finishing breakfast when Morton made his entrance. He got his routine head scratch before I let him outside and filled his food and water dishes.

We were down at the office well before Louie arrived. I made a fresh pot of coffee and sat drinking a mug while looking out the window in search of a black SUV with a bald driver. He never appeared, and I chalked it up to me getting hyper about a new client. Not to mention a *sexy* new client. Just as I watched Louie pull up behind my car, my phone rang.

"Dev Haskell," was how I answered, followed by a sip of coffee.

"Hey, Baby, just checking in. Did you find anything out yesterday?" a woman asked.

"Tracey?"

"Yeah, good morning. Oh, you're not in a meeting or something, are you?"

"No, no, just finished up with a client, and I'm watching him get into his car. I always like to make sure they're safe when they leave."

"Oh, my God. You are so good. What did you find out yesterday?"

"I learned that Percy has a very large office with a lot of high-tech equipment."

"You were actually in his office?" she asked, sounding more than a little surprised.

"Yeah, it's quite the place. He had two other people in there. I'm guessing employees. He does have employees, doesn't he?"

"I think so, but I don't know for sure. They could be contract people, you know, just hired for a specific project for a day, a week, or a month. He never really talked much about what he did all day, every day." She suddenly sounded like she was talking to someone else. "Okay, I'll be there in just a minute. You've got the beach ball?" I heard a man's voice but couldn't make out what he was saying. "Oh, sorry about that. I just wanted to check in and see if you uncovered anything."

Uncovered anything? "I'll keep you posted, Tracey. We both better get back to work. Talk to you later."

"Yeah, let me know if you find out anything," she said and disconnected just as the office door opened, and red-faced Louie stepped in carrying a bakery box. He gave me a wave as he walked around his picnic table and collapsed into his desk chair. He took a couple of minutes to catch his breath, then cleared his throat and said, "Good morning, brought us a little treat. I figured you could use some sweetening." He stepped over and set the box on my desk. "Fresh caramel rolls. They were just arranging them on the tray when I walked in. Check them out," he said and opened the box. There were four cinnamon rolls covered with caramel sauce. "Go ahead, help yourself, Dev."

"Oh, Louie, this is perfect. Thank you," I said, reaching in and taking one of the rolls. It was warm to the touch and slightly sticky. I set it on my desk and licked my fingertips.

"Here, let me top up your coffee," Louie offered and grabbed my mug before I could reply. He topped it up and set the mug in front of me. Then he noticed his mug still off to the side of my desk where Tracey had left it yesterday morning. Fortunately, it was empty of creamy coffee. He filled it up, took a sip, then grabbed a caramel roll and settled in at his picnic table desk. "Mmm-mmm, delicious," he said over a mouthful of caramel roll.

"So, to what do I owe the pleasure?" I asked and nodded at the caramel roll on my desk.

"What? I can't spring for a little treat in the morning just to get our day started off on the right foot?"

I took a bite of the gooey roll. The caramel sauce was still warm enough to leave a sticky drip that landed on my chin. "Thanks for getting these, Louie. What's up?"

"Okay, okay, bear with me. I got a call from a distant acquaintance. He can be a bit of a pain. Let me rephrase that, he can be a major pain, okay? Anyway, he asked me to put in a good word for him and see if you might have some time to check into something. He wouldn't tell me what it was."

"You said the guy was a pain?"

"Yeah, always has been, even when we were in school, but he's been very successful in the business world, and now he's even more full of himself. Pictures himself as a ladies' man. I think women think of him as their bank. I don't know if he's got an employee problem, or he's been hacked, or is he hacking someone. If you don't want to get into it, believe me, I understand."

"Oh, no, I'll be happy to check it out, Louie. I can always tell him no. Give me the contact information, and I'll give him a call."

"Oh, thanks, Dev. Really appreciate it. Just remember, there's no pressure from me if you don't want to take whatever he's got going. Here's his number, and thanks." Louie handed me an envelope with a name and number scrawled on it. He glanced at his watch and said, "I better head down to the courthouse." He crammed the rest of the caramel roll into his mouth, licked his fingertips, and gave me a wave as he headed out the door.

I watched out the window as he climbed into his faded Ford Fiesta and drove away. I took a sip of coffee, looked at the number, and placed a call to Louie's acquaintance, a guy named Ernest Stanton.

Four

The woman answered saying, "Rebel Investments."

"Hi, I'm calling for Ernest Stanton," I said.

"Who may I say is calling?"

"My name is Dev Haskell. I'm replying to a request from Mr. Stanton."

"Please hold while I transfer your call," she said and then did just that, transferring my call before I could even say thank you.

"Mmm, Ernest Stanton, and this is your luck day," a voice said. Then it sounded like he swallowed something.

"Mr. Stanton, my name is Dev Haskell. I'm a private investigator, and I office with an acquaintance of yours, Louie Laufen."

"Humph, Louis. Yes, he mentioned you. I have a bit of a problem here. Would you be available to meet with me sometime this week?"

"I think I can do that. If you want to schedule a day and time, I should be able to adjust my schedule."

"Wonderful, give me a moment, and let me check my calendar. Would you be available tomorrow, Wednesday, at 11:00?"

"I think so. Let me check my schedule. Hold on just a moment, please," I said, then glanced out the window at a young woman pushing a stroller. I watched as she walked around the corner and disappeared behind a hedge. "Yes, sir, thanks for waiting. I can make that."

"Good, we're downtown at 400 Robert Street."

"I know the building," I lied. "I'll see you tomorrow morning at 11:00, sir."

"Looking forward to it, Mr. Haskell. Thank you for the call, and please give my regards to Louis."

"I'll be sure to do that, sir," I said just as he disconnected. I sat back in my chair and thought for a moment about how strange life was, coming from virtually no business to suddenly two new clients in as many days. One of whom paid me upfront in cash. Which reminded me that I wanted to knock on the door where Percy Riggs was renting. I took Morton for a brief walk, and then we drove past Percy's office. Since I saw his car in the parking lot, that gave me the all-clear to knock on the main door of the house where he rented.

Because of the narrow streets in that older section of town, parking was allowed on only one side of the street. Lucky for me, it was the same side that Percy lived on. I pulled in front of the house and parked. Morton had a look on his face suggesting maybe we were going for a walk.

"Sorry, pal. This shouldn't take too long," I said as I locked the doors and headed up the winding brick path to the front door. The door was oak with a large six-foot panel of beveled glass and a brass doorknob. A black, post-mounted mailbox with the image of a pony express rider just below the brass flap labeled 'LETTERS' was bolted down on the front stoop. I pushed the doorbell and heard it chiming inside.

A half-minute later, a woman appeared in the hallway. She was just an inch or two over five feet tall, with neatly arranged brown hair. She wore expensive-looking slacks, a designer blouse, and a string of pearls. She opened the door to the small entry and then said, "Yes?" from behind the beveled glass door.

"Hello, sorry to bother you. Is Percy Riggs home?"

She nodded and said, "Percy lives up on the third floor."

I shook my head and placed a hand behind my right ear, signaling I was having trouble hearing her.

She repeated herself, only louder.

I gave the same signal with my hand behind my ear, only this time I said, "I'm sorry, I can't hear you."

She gave a somewhat disgusted look, hooked a brass chain to the beveled glass door, and then unlocked the door and opened it no more than an inch. "I said, Percy lives up on the third floor."

"Oh, okay, sorry to bother you. Is this his entrance? I'm just in town for the day, and he told me that he had moved here recently."

"His entrance is around the side, but I'm sure he's at his office. He seems to work eternally."

"Yeah, that sounds like Percy. I have his office address on my GPS. I'm sorry to bother you. Ummm, if he's not home, is it possible to leave a note at his door?"

"Well, the door heading up to his apartment will be locked, but there's a mail slot you could drop the note through."

"All right, again, I'm sorry to bother you. Thank you for your time."

"Shall I tell him you stopped by?"

"No, I've got an hour. I can head over to his office. If I remember, it's on Hampden Avenue North in the Midway district." She nodded. "Anyway, I've got the address on my GPS. Thank you, and have a nice day," I said. I gave her a wave as I stepped off the front stoop and walked back to my car. She continued to watch me until I drove away.

I drove a block over to Grand Avenue, took a right, and two blocks later took a left onto Dale Street. A block later, I drove down Summit Avenue, one of the nation's most famous Victorian mansion streets. Four blocks later, I took a right and headed down Ramsey Hill to the entrance to 35E. I had just pulled onto the entrance and was checking my side-view mirror. The lane next to me was clear of traffic, but as I pulled onto the freeway, I caught the momentary image of a black SUV pulled to the curb just before the entrance ramp. No one ever stops there. Was it the same SUV that I thought was following me yesterday? There was no way to tell, so I accelerated and then checked my rearview mirror a half-dozen times as I sped to the Randolph Avenue exit. I never did see the SUV and decided it probably wasn't the bald guy from yesterday.

I drove down Randolph to my building, made a U-turn at the intersection with The Spot bar, and parked just across the street from my office. I sat in the car for ten minutes to see if the black SUV would appear. It never did, so Morton and I headed up to the office.

Five

L ouie was back by mid-afternoon. I watched as he parked behind my car. I emptied what remained from the coffee pot into his mug and turned the burner off. Along with the stairs creaking, I heard a couple of groans as he made his way up to the second floor. A moment later, the office door opened. Red-faced Louie stepped in and gave me a wave. He set his briefcase on the picnic table, grabbed a caramel roll from the box, and collapsed into his desk chair.

"I saw you pull up and just poured you a coffee, Louie."

He flashed me the OK sign and sipped his coffee for a few minutes. His cough sounded like the side of a mountain collapsing, but he eventually managed to ask, "Were you able to get in touch with Ernest?"

"Yeah, we talked on the phone, for just a minute and I've got an 11:00 appointment with him tomorrow morning. He sends his regards. I didn't mention your cough and cold."

"Oh, well, thanks for getting in touch with him and for not mentioning this damn cough and cold. It would just become one more subject he could lecture me on."

"He seemed like a nice enough guy on the phone."

"That's because he wants something from you. God only knows what."

"Maybe he wants some advice," Louie shot me a look. "Then again . . ."

"Yeah, don't expect that. At the end of the day, he's an authority on whatever subject you'll be discussing. I could tell you he's more than a little strange but that said, there's no disputing the fact that he's very successful."

"Well, guess I'll see how he is tomorrow. How'd your court appearance go?"

"Pretty much by the book. Since it's a first offense, my client has a restricted license for one year. He's to attend AA meetings, and his car insurance will go through the roof. But he doesn't have to spend weekends or nights locked up. He's got all the earmarkings of a guy who'll learn his lesson after this."

"He's lucky to have you representing him."

"It's just so sad, another guy over-served and driving home, and he gets nailed. Amazing, in a way that it's what my business is."

I was about to say something when my phone rang, Tracey Wilde. "Oh, I better take this."

"Is it Ernie?"

I shook my head and answered. "Hi Tracey, how are things?"

"Hi Dev, they're going okay. I was wondering if you might have time to meet me for dinner. Nothing fancy. In fact, if you wanted, we could eat at that Spot hangout you go to."

"Oh, thanks, Tracey. The only problem is they don't serve food, so we'd be on the liquid diet."

"I could do that, I think."

"Well, I'd better not. How about this, we could meet at Shamrock's. Do you know where that is? They've got great burgers. It's a nice friendly place."

"It's down on West Seventh, isn't it?"

"Yeah, that's right. What's your schedule like?"

"I'm free anytime. We finished shooting pictures and filming for today. I need to get cleaned up, but how 'bout if we met there at, say, 6:30?"

"Works for me," I said. "First one there gets the table, okay?"

"I'll see you there," she said and disconnected.

"That's your woman getting ready to pull the trigger on a divorce?"

"Yeah, I've done some checking. Thus far, the only thing I've been able to come up with is the guy is working all the time. I haven't found anything online. Nothing court-related on him in the city or county. I spoke to him for all of five seconds, but he seemed like a nice guy."

Louie shook his head. "It never seems to end. He's probably exactly the same guy he was when they got married, but now she's unhappy."

"That sounds a little far-fetched. You know, some-times things simply don't work out, Louie. I've only started looking into the guy. To tell you the truth, I hope I don't find anything, but we'll see. Anyway, I'm going to grab dinner with her tonight. It will be interesting to see if she shows up on time. I have the feeling she's one of those people that is routinely late. If you're getting together, you tell her 6:30 and make the reservation for 7:15."

"Well, if you're heading out to dinner at 6:30, would you care to join me at The Spot for one?"

I thought about that for a minute, then shook my head. "No, thanks, but I'd better take a pass. I should take Morton home and get him settled in. You planning on coming in tomorrow morning?"

Louie nodded. "Yeah, I need to get back on sched-ule."

Six

Louie headed over to The Spot, and I took Morton on a little longer walk than usual. I stayed on the lookout but never saw the black SUV. Once home, I hit the shower, then pulled on a clean pair of jeans and a short sleeve shirt. I was down at Shamrock's ten minutes early and scored the last empty booth in the main room. No need to hurry. Tracey had set the 6:30 meetup time and then waltzed in promptly at a little after 7:00. Based on the head-turning she caused as she strutted in, she was worth the wait.

"Hi Dev, been here long?" she asked as she leaned over, kissed my cheek, then nibbled my ear lobe and gave a sexy growl.

"I beat you by just a couple of minutes," I lied, deciding the thirty minutes were worth it since I got the nibble and the little sexy growl.

She slid into the booth across from me, looked around, and said, "God, I can't remember the last time I was in here."

"I've always liked this place. It's laid back, has good food, and invariably I run into someone I know here."

"Probably not the place to be if you were seeing someone on the side," she said.

I didn't react but made a mental note. "How'd your day go? You sounded busy. Were you doing a model shoot? Some new outfits or something?"

She shook her head and laughed. "Always with the jokes. We were finishing up a series of ads for the fourth video in the series. They'll be doing the editing over the next week, and then we run preorders for two weeks, email our mailing list, and then release and cross our fingers."

"Preorders? People pay for your pictures?"

She nodded. "Yes, we sell packets of images, greeting cards, and of course, the video. Along with those items, we, umm, instruct on everything from makeup to certain exercises and some health recommendations. We've developed quite a following over the last two years, but like any business, things are constantly changing. You have to do that if you want to keep up."

"Hi, can I get you something from the bar?" the server asked as she stepped up to the table. She looked like a twenty-year-old college kid.

"Tracey?" I asked.

"I think I'll have a glass of your Sauvignon Blanc."

"Sir?"

"I'll have a Summit IPA."

"I'll be back in just a moment," the server promised as she placed two menus on the table.

"You know what you're going to get?" I asked.

"I'll have to look. What are you getting? You sound like you already know."

"I get the same thing every time, a bourbon bacon chicken sandwich."

"Oh, interesting," she said, not sounding all that impressed.

The server was back a moment later with our drinks. As she set the glass of wine in front of Tracey, she asked, "Have you had a chance to look at the menu?"

Tracey nodded and said, "I'll have a half-order of the chicken salad."

"And sir?"

"I'll take the bourbon bacon chicken sandwich with fries."

"I'll put your orders in. It shouldn't be long," she said and hurried off.

"So, what have you found out about Percy?" Tracey asked and followed up with a sip of wine. She took one of those sips where she set the glass down as soon as the wine touched her lips.

I took a couple of gulps from my beer mug and set it off to the side. "All the background information thus far places him in the category of a 'nice guy.' I haven't discovered anything even remotely criminal. No arrests, no charges. Not so much as a parking ticket. I mentioned I was in his office. I was there for all of about fifteen seconds, but he couldn't have been nicer. I told him I was looking for a friend and thought he worked in the office where Percy was located. Percy offered to look up the company. There were two other people working there. The place looked very high-tech."

"Well, yes, of course, after all, that's his business. With the way you're describing him, are you suggesting my divorce could be denied?"

"Oh, no, nothing like that. It will be granted if that's what you want. It's just that, at this point, unless I find something else, it won't be granted on the basis of him having an affair or physical abuse."

"What does that mean as far as me selling the house?"

"You're selling your house?"

"I'm selling the one he and I lived in, not the one where I live now."

"I would think you can sell the house. Depending on the contract, you may have to split the profits fifty-fifty with him."

She shook her head. "I don't want to do that."

"Yeah, I get that, but the court system is required to treat both parties fairly. Do you think he's been having an affair with someone? Or is he doing something illegal?"

She shook her head. "No, unfortunately, he's not wired that way. He's a very straight shooter."

The server arrived with our meals. Tracey's half-salad was in a small bowl and came with a plate holding four crackers. It was almost too small to be considered an hors d'oeuvre. "Mmm-mmm, perfect," she said and took a bite from one of the crackers.

My bourbon bacon chicken sandwich was about five inches high, with a couple of pounds of french fries piled across the rest of the platter. "Feel free to help yourself to some fries," I said.

The waitress smiled and asked, "Will there be anything else?"

We both shook our heads. As soon as she left, Tracey reached over and grabbed a french fry. "Mmm-mmm, very good."

"Like I said, help yourself." We were quiet for the next few minutes. Tracey inhaled her half-salad and then started in on my french fries one at a time. I was working my way through the bourbon bacon chicken sandwich and didn't care.

I had just finished my sandwich. Tracey was still working on my french fries when a guy I didn't recognize stepped over to our booth and said, "Tracey, could I talk to you, please?"

She got a shocked look on her face and said, "No, Davy, this is not a good time. I'm in the middle of a business meeting, and I—"

"It will only take a minute."

"Not now. You can call me if you—"

"I just need to—"

"Excuse me," I said. "But we're in the middle of a business meeting and—"

"I wasn't talking to you," he said and gave me a look.

I felt my blood surge, and I had to hold onto the edge of the table before I grabbed him from behind and slammed his thick head into the side of the booth.

"Davy, please leave. I don't want to talk with you right now. Call me tomorrow."

"Okay, just make sure you answer my call," he said. He gave me another look before he hurried toward the door.

I was tempted to follow, but Tracey said, "Thank you for not getting involved, Dev. I'm sorry, he just never seems to learn."

"What is he, some guy you dated? A former customer?"

She shook her head and grabbed another french fry. "No, he does photo shots for me. He's an excellent photographer. I'll give him that much. But I'm striking poses and smiling, and he's suddenly thinking we're in a relationship. We have a business relationship," she said but didn't explain any further.

"He strikes me as the type that, no matter how many times you tell him 'no,' he's going to think, 'If I just ask her one more time.' Watch yourself. I've dealt with that type before. He'll convince himself you need to be rescued, and he's the only one who can do it."

"God, I certainly don't need that kind of headache."

We chatted for another ten minutes, which convinced me that Davy the jerk had thrown a wet blanket on any chance of something positive happening later that night. I paid the bill and walked Tracey to her coupe. I got a quick peck on the cheek for my effort and watched her drive off. I was home in time to catch the news with Morton, after which we wandered up to bed.

Seven

Louie stepped into the office the following morning and asked, "So, how did your evening go?" I gave him a thumbs-down and a short version of the night. As I talked, I emptied what was left of the coffee into my mug. It filled the mug just slightly over halfway and had a smell confirming it had been on the burner since yesterday. In the event I had any doubt, one sip convinced me that was the case. I turned the burner off. As I made a fresh pot, I reminded Louie that I had an 11:00 appointment with his friend, Ernest Stanton.

"Good luck with that. Like I said yesterday, he's the authority on whatever subject you'd care to discuss. Oh, and let me stress, he's an acquaintance, not a friend."

"Well, it will be interesting to see what's up. He didn't mention anything on the phone yesterday except to set the appointment."

"Classic Ernie. He's putting himself in charge. Your job is to realize that and follow his instructions to the letter."

"We'll see. Are you going to be here this morning?"

Louie shook his head. "I'm due in court at 11:00. I'll be out of here a little after 10:00."

I dumped my mug of burnt coffee down the sink and said, "I'll take Morton for a walk. I've no idea how long my meeting with this Stanton guy is going to go." I took the leash from the hook, which immediately got Morton's attention. He was up and at the door with his tail wagging. We headed out of the office and took our usual route. I checked a couple of times for the black SUV but never saw it. We were back in the office fifteen minutes later. "You mind if I steal one of your legal pads?"

Louie shook his head again and said, "No, go ahead and help yourself."

"I figure I'd better be prepared to take notes during Stanton's lecture."

Louie chuckled and said, "Don't be surprised if he has a printed outline that you'll be able to follow as he proceeds with his instructions. The guy should have been a college professor."

"That doesn't sound very good to me."

"Just follow the precise directions, and you'll be fine."

I placed the legal pad in my computer bag, set my laptop in the bag, and drove downtown to Rebel Investments. The downtown area of the city is no different than every other city in the country. It's been in the midst of change since before the year 2000. The advent of the internet only sped things up. It's no longer necessary for businesses to be located downtown. Whether it's a legal firm, a retail outlet, or a publishing house, with people having to work from home during the pandemic, the departure of businesses from downtown only increased. If they didn't depart, there was an awfully good chance that they were reducing their office space. Employees were no longer working forty hours per week in an office cubicle. Now they were working from home a good deal of any week. So it seemed with the building where Rebel Investments was located.

At 10:45 on a weekday morning, I was able to park on Robert Street a half-block away from the building. That would have been impossible even just three years ago. I passed two more open parking places on the street as I walked toward the building.

The structure was sixteen stories tall. The exterior of the first three floors was covered with a buff-colored stone, and everything was tinted glass from there to the top. I walked into the large lobby and headed for a bank of four elevators. The doors opened on one of the elevators just as I approached, and two women stepped off. I stepped on and pushed the button for the fifteenth floor. Nondescript music played softly in the background as the elevator rose almost to the top floor. I stepped off, and much like the building where Technical Percy was located, there was an empty office directly in front of the elevator. Rebel Investments was two doors down the hall.

The door was glass with the name Rebel Investments and, below that, the office number 1504. I opened the door and stepped into a neat lobby with a couch, coffee table, and two matching wingback chairs off to the right. The carpet felt plush beneath my feet. Straight ahead was a reception counter topped with white marble. The receptionist behind the counter smiled and greeted me, "Good morning. How may I help you?"

"Hi, my name is Dev Haskell. I have an 11:00 appointment to see Ernest Stanton."

She smiled. "If you'd like to take a seat, I'll let Mr. Stanton know that you're here."

"Thank you," I replied and headed for one of the wingback chairs. There was a large painting in an elaborate frame of an older gentleman standing in front of a fireplace. He was holding a roll of paper with a red wax seal, it looked like a classic sort of document from the 1700s. He was bald with gray hair along the sides. There was just the slightest hint of a halo above his head. As I sat down, I could see the receptionist talking on the phone but couldn't hear what she was saying.

She nodded, smiled, and hung up the phone. "Someone will be here in a moment to escort you," she said and then began sorting documents at the counter.

A minute later, a woman stepped out of the door next to the reception counter and called, "Mr. Haskell?" as if there were ten other people in the lobby. Other than the receptionist, I was the only person. I waved and headed toward her. "If you will follow me, please, I'll take you back to Mr. Stanton's office." We walked down a hallway with six offices, three on either side. Each office was occupied by an individual, most of whom were on the phone. We walked past a large area with a dozen cubicles separated by six-foot-high sections that were covered in blue fabric. Four offices with glass walls overlooked the cubicles. Just beyond the four offices were two larger offices, one of which was labeled 'Ernest Stanton, CEO' in gold letters and carved trim around the door frame.

The woman knocked on the door as she opened it, directing me to step in with a nod of her head. A large bald man with glasses and gray wisps of hair on the sides of his head studied me from behind his desk. The desk was clear, with the exception of a keyboard, a telephone, and a crystal bowl of foil wrapped chocolates. A large desktop monitor was off to the side.

"Thank you, Eileen, that will be all. Mr. Haskell, it's nice to finally meet you. Thank you for coming," Stanton said as he rose from behind his elegant antique carved desk. His glasses had wide black frames. He was approximately my height and a good two hundred pounds heavier. His white shirt was starched, and his blue suit looked immaculate with a blue and white houndstooth tie and matching silk pocket square. A number of chins hung over the tie knot.

"It's nice to meet you, Mr. Stanton. I have to say you have a very lovely office here. How many people do you have on staff?"

He smiled and said, "Thirty-four and counting. Just like everywhere, we have a number of open positions we've been trying to fill, but finding qualified people is next to impossible in today's world." He shook my hand and then nodded toward one of the leather chairs in front of his desk. "Please take a seat."

As I sat down, Stanton groaned as he settled in behind his desk. "I have to ask, how is Louis doing?"

"He's doing very well. He stays busy, constantly getting new clients. He's the go-to attorney in town for certain charges."

"Mmm-hmm, dealing with the lower strata of society. I'm afraid I'll never understand it."

"Well, everyone has the right to representation," I said as I pulled the legal pad and a pen from my computer bag.

"Yes, but a lower class of individuals. He could be making so much more." I decided not to mention that the odds were at least one of Stanton's employees had probably faced DWI charges at some point. "Tell me about your endeavors, Haskell."

"I work on a variety of different cases. I've investigated murders, assaults, extra-marital affairs, employment records, companies, frankly all sorts of things, and just when I think I've seen it all, something brand new pops up."

"Does the name Gretchen Donahue ring a bell with you?"

I thought about that for a moment, then slowly shook my head. "I can't say that it does." I wrote the name down on the legal pad.

"I'll take that as a positive note," Stanton said. He opened a desk drawer and pulled out a sheet of paper. "I'd like you to research this individual's history. Her name, address, email, and private phone number are here. Beyond that, I'll be interested in whatever you find out."

I glanced at the paper. That was all that was on it, general information you could have gotten from the phone book if they were published anymore.

"Questions?" Stanton asked.

"Not really, sir. Are you under any timeline for this information?"

"Not urgently, but obviously sooner rather than later. She's been, mmm-mmm, lingering around a client's business, and I'm mildly curious."

"Do you know, is she a competitor, a disgruntled customer of a client, or maybe an attorney?"

He shook his head. "I've no idea, Mr. Haskell."

"Is she employed locally?"

"I believe so, but maybe broaden your investigation statewide. As far as time goes, today is Wednesday. What if we say we'll meet again a week from today?"

"Yes, sir, that will work," I said.

"Excellent. I expect that you will adhere to the client privilege aspect and not mention any of this to Louis."

"Not a problem, sir."

"Good, well, don't let me detain you from starting your investigation, Mr. Haskell," Stanton said as he groaned to his feet and extended his hand, basically telling me to get out of his office and get to work. I smiled and headed out the door, bringing our two-minute meeting to a close.

Eight

I was back in the office thirty minutes later and online looking up Gretchen Donahue. The name was more common than I realized. Fortunately, with her address, I quickly nailed it down to the woman in question. There was very little information online. No images I could find other than an image of her home on Google Maps.

She apparently lived in a two-story structure on West James Avenue in St. Paul. The house was about three blocks from the campus of St. Catherine University. The school, at one time, was a Catholic woman's college, although I didn't know if that was still the case. Yes, it was still Catholic and operated by the Sisters of St. Joseph, but I think it had merged, at least on the basis of students, with St. Thomas University, formerly a Catholic boys' college. Anyway, I had a picture of her home.

Louie was still out, so I grabbed the leash and took Morton for a walk. I kept my eye out for the black SUV, which fortunately never appeared. When we finished the walk, I put Morton in the car and drove past Gretchen Donahue's home on West James Avenue.

At no surprise, it looked just like the image on Google Maps. Given the neighborhood, I guessed the place had been built in the late 1930s. I slowed as I went past the buff-colored, two-story structure with white trim and a dark red front door. Two side-by-side windows were on either side of the front door, with flower boxes beneath each window. Two single-window dormers with a peaked roof were on either end of the roof. A couple of steps led up to a brick porch across the front of the house with two wrought iron benches and a two foot high wrought iron railing. The place looked well-manicured, with a very large tree stump on the left half of the front lawn, suggesting a recently removed tree.

I drove down the street, took a right at the corner, and drove up the alley. Donahue's place had a single-car garage that appeared original to the home. The garage door was up, and a white Volkswagen Atlas was parked in the garage. I slowed to take a closer look just as the taillights lit up, signaling the car was about to back up. I quickly got the license plate number and headed down the alley. The Volkswagen backed out of the garage and drove down the alley in the opposite direction. I turned onto the street at the end of the alley, stopped, and wrote down the license plate number on a receipt from McDonald's. I drove around the block and headed back up the alley. The garage door was closed. The backyard was surrounded by a six-foot fence, and what looked like an apple tree stood next to the garage in the back of the lot. I headed back out of the alley, drove past St. Catherine University, and down Randolph Avenue to the office.

Louie was seated at his desk when we returned.

"Oh, just back from your meeting with Ernie? You didn't take Morton, did you?"

"No, I was back for a bit. We went on a walk and then drove past the home of someone your pal Stanton has me checking out."

"Remember, he's not my pal. If he has you checking someone out, it could be a potential investor. Actually, that could turn out to be a very good opportunity for both of you. You could see if the person is above board and, in the process, theoretically, eliminate some potential risks for Ernie and the company. How did your meeting go, anyway?"

"About what you said, he was very pleasant, but I had the distinct impression he didn't have a lot of time to waste. We met for all of two minutes. He gave me an individual's name and has me checking them out."

"Any idea what for?"

"This is the point where I'm supposed to state attorney-client privilege, even though I'm not an attorney."

"Or privileged, for that matter, but I get it. Good luck, maybe he'll turn into a regular client, and you'll end up checking out all sorts of people for him."

"That's what I'm hoping."

I went back online and checked out the county records. The property taxes on Gretchen Donahue's place were up to date. She wasn't listed on any financial warning sites. I googled her name and versions of her name on various business and Google sites but didn't come up with anything.

An hour later, Louie turned off his computer and pushed his desk chair away from the picnic table. "Can I talk the two of you into a beverage at our semi-private club across the street?"

"Since I'm not coming up with anything online, I think that might be a very good idea. Let me just shut down here, and we'll join you," I said. I turned off my computer, locked my desk drawer, and grabbed Morton's leash. He was off his pillow in a nanosecond, and the three of us headed over to The Spot. Louie ordered the first round, along with a bag of pork rinds. He'd just handed a handful to Morton when Mike arrived with our drinks. Before I could grab my beer mug, my phone rang. Tracey's name flashed across my screen.

"Oh, sorry. Let me just take this outside. Back in a minute," I said and stepped out the side door. "Hi, Tracey. What's up? Everything okay?"

"No, Dev, I've got a real problem," she said. Her words sounded slurred.

"Why? What happened?"

"I have a gorgeous dinner arranged for friends, and they just called and can't make it. I desperately need someone to come over for dinner. I promise to show my appreciation if you can make it."

My heart started to pound after that last statement. "Oh, man, I'd love to help you out. Umm, can I bring something? A bottle of wine, dessert, or maybe an hors d'oeuvre?"

"A bottle of wine since I'm almost out and your sexy self would be wonderful. The sooner you get here, the better."

"Oh, Tracey, don't go to any trouble. Listen, I'll see you shortly. You sure I can't bring you something else?"

"Yeah, really sure. Did I ever give you my address?"

"You did, but I'm not in my office. I'm just finishing up a meeting. Give me your address again, please."

She told me her address, twice. I thanked her and hurried into The Spot, repeating the address.

"Everything okay?" Louie asked as he set his drink down.

I nodded, repeated the address once more, then grabbed a coaster from the stack on the bar, turned it over, and wrote it down. "A client. I have to stop over and see her, umm, I mean him. God, sorry, but I can only stay for one."

"What are you sorry for, Dev? Last week you were sleeping in your office chair or watching a movie on your computer. Now, suddenly, you don't have enough time in the day. That's the right kind of problem to have."

"Yeah, I guess you're right," I agreed, and we clinked glasses. I finished my beer in record time. Morton and I drove home five minutes later. I let Morton out into the backyard and then hurried upstairs. I shaved, washed my hands, and slipped on a not-too-wrinkled shirt. I encouraged Morton back into the house with a biscuit and filled his water dish. I grabbed a bottle of white wine from the refrigerator and hurried out to my car.

Nine

Tracey's new house was just across the river from St. Paul in the town of Mendota. It was only a fifteen-minute drive from my place. She lived in a condominium association, in one of a dozen unattached units positioned around a man-made pond. Her blue coupe was parked in the driveway, and I spotted it as soon as I turned the corner. All the units were single-story brick units with cream-colored trim. I pulled to the curb in front of her place, grabbed the bottle of chilled wine, and hurried up the driveway, past the coupe, and rang the doorbell.

She opened the door thirty seconds later, holding a glass of wine and grinning. She wore very tight white shorts and a white, textured, striped tee shirt that exposed a bare midriff. The lack of a bra was apparent, not that I was complaining.

She grinned, took a healthy sip of wine, and said, "Oh, Dev. Thanks for coming on such short notice." She leaned over and gave me a kiss on the cheek. Did she purposely brush against me? Once again, not a complaint.

"Thanks for the invitation, Tracey. Here, I brought you a bottle of wine."

"Oh, you shouldn't have, but glad you did. Come on in." She emptied the glass in her hand and headed toward the kitchen. Her shorts were low cut, and as I followed her through the living room, I examined the tattoo that read, 'Please, Sir,' across her lower back, an inch or two below her waistline. I looked for the outline of a thong on her shorts but couldn't detect one.

She led me into the kitchen. There was a stack of paper plates on the granite-topped counter in the middle of the room. Next to the paper plates was a wine bottle with about a half-inch of wine remaining. Next to the wine bottle were two boxes labeled Pizza Hut. She set my wine bottle on the counter next to the almost empty bottle.

"Hope you like pizza, baby. There's plenty here," Tracey said. She emptied the remnants of the open bottle into her glass and then twisted the cap off the bottle I brought and topped up her glass, mixing the two wines. I decided it probably wouldn't make a difference since she'd apparently already been over-served. "So, Dev, honey, how did your day go?"

"Good, thanks for asking. I picked up a new client, and hopefully, that will lead to some potential for a lot more business. How was your day?"

"Absolutely wonderful. Finished the project we've been working on for the past week." She raised her wine glass in a salute and took two healthy swallows. "We'll put the finishing touches on the marketing plan. We've got ads scheduled, and I've got the next two days off to do whatever I want to do. You know what I'd like to do to you?" she asked just as her phone rang.

"Oh, for the love of— Hey, I'm just in the middle of something. Can I call you back tomorrow?" she said as she strolled out of the room with her glass of wine. I waited a couple of minutes and then peeked into the living room.

I could hear her voice but couldn't make out what was being said. Her bare feet were resting on the back of one of the two couches positioned on either side of her fireplace. Above the fireplace was a framed painting, probably four feet high and three feet wide. The painting, in a gold gilt frame, was of a naked, dark-haired woman in the post-impressionist style. Her back was facing toward the artist, exposing a lower back tattoo identical to the one I'd seen on Tracey just a moment ago. Obviously, the painting was of her. It was attractive, I guess. I mean, she was certainly beautiful, and I figured the tattoo was probably unique.

I stepped back into the kitchen and poured myself a glass of wine. I took a sip and looked around the kitchen. There were black granite countertops, white cabinets with silver handles and drawer pulls, a brushed chrome refrigerator, and a seven-burner black stove with two ovens. I opened the refrigerator just to take a peek. There was a half-gallon of milk, a small round box labeled brie cheese, and a half-filled container of cherry tomatoes. All the other shelves were empty.

I closed the door and peeked back into the living room. Her bare feet were still resting on the back of the couch. I took a sip of wine and raised the lids on the pizza boxes. My stomach immediately growled. One pizza appeared to be about five different kinds of cheese, and the other looked like sausage, onion, and peppers. The smell was delicious.

I glanced into the living room. Tracey's feet were in the same position. I figured that since the call was taking longer than expected, it wouldn't hurt to steal a slice of pizza. I grabbed a piece of the sausage pizza and took a bite. It was delicious, and my stomach growled once more. I quickly ate the piece and tossed the crust into the wastebasket beneath the kitchen sink. I debated taking another piece but figured I'd wait for Tracey to finish her call.

Five minutes later, I stepped to the kitchen door and glanced into the living room. Tracey's feet were still up on the back of the couch. I strained my ears but couldn't hear her talking. I waited a long moment, then stepped over toward the couch, thinking I'd give her a sign and ask if I could bring her some pizza. I leaned over and stared.

Her eyes were closed, and she was breathing deeply. Her cell phone was upside down on the floor, and the empty wine glass was lying on her bare stomach. Even passed out, she was still attractive. I reached over and gently shook her shoulder. "Tracey, Tracey," I said.

She slapped my hand away, mumbled something I couldn't understand, and then rolled over on her side with her face against the back of the couch. I quickly grabbed her empty wine glass just before it disappeared. I thought for a minute and decided there was nothing I could do. I set her wine glass on the coffee table, picked up her cell phone, and placed it next to the wine glass. I stared for a moment, shook my head, and went back into the kitchen.

I ate three more pieces of the sausage pizza and two pieces of the cheese pizza. I took a plate from the cupboard, put two of the crusts on the plate, and placed it out on the coffee table next to Tracey, still passed out on the couch. I stared at her for another long moment, shook my head, and went back into the kitchen. There was a box of chocolate-covered ice cream cones in the freezer drawer at the bottom of the refrigerator. I opened the box, unwrapped an ice cream cone, and strolled back out to the living room. Tracey was snoring now and dead to the world.

I debated waking her up, but that immediately struck me as a bad idea. The odds of her being in a crabby mood outweighed any potential benefits. I wandered down the hallway and into what appeared to be a combination office and TV room.

A desk was positioned in front of a double window overlooking a large pond. A brick patio with two lawn chairs and a fire pit was spread out behind the house. At the end of the patio was a small hedge, and beyond that, a massive flower garden with a half-dozen rose trees and all sorts of flowers growing all the way down to the pond. At the moment, eight or ten ducks were swimming across the pond.

The desk was an 'L' shaped contemporary affair on metal legs with a Formica top and a pull-out shelf with a keyboard and a mouse. A large iMac desktop computer rested on the desk. A flat screen was mounted on the wall opposite the desk. Behind the desk and mounted on the wall were six 8 1/2 X 11 framed, color photos of Tracey. Other than the one photo where she was wearing a red lace negligee that left nothing to the imagination, she was naked. Two of the images had her positioned against a large wooden headboard. She was posing next to a fireplace with a fire in another image. The last two pictures had her stepping out of a walk-in shower and reaching for a white towel, and the final one had her topless and sponging off the hood of the blue coupe parked out in the driveway.

Naked Tracey was gorgeous. No complaint there. It just struck me as unusual that she would have the images framed and on the wall of her office. The photos were clearly professionally taken, and based on her hairstyle and appearance, I guessed they were relatively recent, probably taken within the past month or two. I stepped out of the office and into the bedroom next to it. The first thing I saw was the king-sized bed that had been in the photos. Once again, the double windows looked out onto the patio, with the flowers and pond beyond. A double-drawer dresser and a makeup table matched the style of the wooden headboard. The en suite bathroom was the same as the photograph, all white with a beautiful deep tub set in front of the double windows looking out at the patio and pond. The walk-in shower from the photo was on the far wall, and just like the photo, there were two white bath towels hanging on the rack next to the shower door.

The tub would easily fit two and had Jacuzzi water jets. It was large enough that I would be able to stretch out and soak with water up to my shoulders. There were two white inflatable pillows attached to either end of the tub, suggesting that Tracey probably did just that, stretching out on a regular basis. A door led out to the hallway.

I looked into the guest room across the hall from the bathroom. The bed was queen-sized, and there was another table with a makeup mirror. I walked back out to the living room. Tracey was still asleep on the couch, lying on her side and snoring. Her tight shorts had slipped down slightly, and I noticed that the 'Please, Sir' tattoo had a red heart at the beginning and the end and was underlined by a line of flowers. She'd be attractive without the tattoo, but the statement and the art seemed to add something. I wondered what the tattoo would look like forty-five years from now.

I headed into the kitchen, closed the lids on the pizza boxes, and looked around for any mess. I quietly shut the front door, double-checked to make sure it was locked and climbed into my car.

Ten

Fifteen minutes later I pulled in front of the office and walked over to The Spot. "Oh, look who's back," Mike called from behind the bar. "Get you a beer, Dev?"

"Yeah, and better give Louie a refill while you're at it," I said and headed down the bar.

"That didn't take long. I thought you were gone for the night. Everything go all right with your client?" Louie asked.

I nodded and said, "Yeah, he had some questions, and I just wanted to put him at ease. Sorry I had to run off like that." I didn't want to mention Tracey.

Louie shook his head. "Unless you're self-employed, no one understands why we're on call twenty-four-seven."

"You got that right. Anyway, everything worked out, and if I hadn't gone over tonight, he'd be calling me tomorrow morning at 6:00," I lied.

Mike arrived with my beer and Louie's drink. We chatted back and forth about everything and nothing for the next hour. I had another beer, but Louie took a pass on fresh drink because he didn't want to end up sleeping in his car again. I was home just after 9:00 and caught the evening news before I made my way upstairs to bed. I dreamt of Tracey serving me pizza and wearing just a smile. I was up before the alarm went off, hit the shower, and had been downstairs for forty-five minutes before Morton made his appearance. I gave him a head scratch and let him outside.

We were down in the office before Louie. I made a fresh pot of coffee and was watching the two women in the apartment across the street with my binoculars. When I saw Louie pull up and park his Ford Fiesta behind my car, I put the binoculars back in my desk drawer, turned on my computer, and filled Louie's coffee mug with fresh coffee. I began searching online for anything on Gretchen Donahue, the woman Louie's acquaintance, Ernest Stanton, wanted me to check out. I heard the stairs creaking as Louie made his way up to the office. When he opened the door, I said, "Good morning, Louie. Fresh mug of coffee waiting for you on your desk."

He nodded, set his briefcase on the picnic table, and settled into his desk chair. After a couple of minutes, I asked, "You make it home okay last night?"

"Yeah, not a bother. How 'bout you?"

"The same. Watched the news and went to bed. I'm going to be doing some checking on Tracey Wilde's soon-to-be ex later today, so I won't be able to join you at The Spot tonight. He apparently works late, and I'm going to confirm that over the course of the next few nights."

"Well, you'll be sorely missed."

"Mmm-mmm, the downside of getting busy, I guess." I took the McDonald's receipt with Gretchen Donahue's license plate number out of my wallet and called Dave McGovern over at the state office building.

"McGovern," he answered.

"Hi Dave, Dev Haskell, I—"

"Oh, God, what poor woman are you checking out now?"

"Actually, it is a woman, but I'm not checking her out. Well, at least not the way you're suggesting. Her name is Gretchen Donahue, and she's driving a white Volkswagen Atlas."

"You got a license number?"

"Yeah, I do," I said and read off the plate number.

"Let me put it in and see what—Here we go, yeah, a white Volkswagen Atlas, a 2018. You need an address or a phone number?" I read the address off to him. "That's correct. Phone number?" I read off the phone number on Ernest Stanton's shortlist. "Yeah, that's her home number. You need the office number?"

"Can't hurt if you got it." He read her office number to me. "Does it say where she's employed?"

"Yeah, she works for the state. That phone number is for the State Attorney General's Office. Hey Dev, they're not checking you out, are they?"

"No, thank God," I laughed.

"That's good. I don't need to know how you're dealing with her, but she's a part of the state's Financial Crimes Task Force. My advice is don't screw with those folks."

"Not to worry, it was just a traffic accident. No one was hurt, and fortunately, I wasn't involved."

"Good, no one needs a hassle with those folks. Anything else you need?"

"No, that should do it. As always, much appreciated, Dave."

"You take care," he said and disconnected.

Louie was focused on his desktop computer, which was probably a good thing. I wondered if Ernest Stanton possibly had a client that was under financial investigation. But that didn't make any sense. If he had a client like that, he would cooperate with the state. He'd have to, and given his business, he probably already had more than once. So did that mean the State Attorney General's Office was investigating Stanton?

I thought for a minute and then got up from my desk and grabbed Morton's leash. Morton jumped from his pillow and stood with his nose against the door, wagging his tail.

"You taking him for a walk?" Louie asked as he stared at his computer screen.

"Yeah, back in fifteen minutes," I said and opened the door. We stepped out of the building and headed down the street on our usual route. Once we turned the corner, I pulled out my phone and hit the speed dial button for my pal Aaron LaZelle in the St. Paul Police Department. He headed up the homicide unit, and I didn't think he'd have any information on Gretchen Donahue, but there was a chance he might know someone who would. Aaron answered on the fourth ring.

"No, Dev, whether it's a parking ticket or a speeding ticket, I can't do anything about it," was how he answered.

"Not to worry, Aaron, I just hit the gas, and they couldn't keep up with me, so I'm okay."

"God, not even funny. What's cooking?"

"I've got kind of a goofy deal. A client asked me to check out someone. He wanted any and all information I could find. Without giving you his name, let me just say he's a wealthy guy who does investments. Anyway, it turns out the name he gave me is an investigator for the State Attorney General's Office and is part of the Financial Crimes Task Force. Would you happen to know anyone I could talk to who might be wise to an ongoing investigation? I don't need to know specifics, but if this guy is up to something, I'll back out of the investigation in a heartbeat."

"Mmm-mmm, can't say as I blame you. Are you aware of anything this guy could be involved in?"

"No, I really don't have any idea. I was thinking this was a standard request to check out a potential investor, but once I got wind of the financial fraud thing and my client runs an investment company, I'm thinking I may not want to get anywhere near this."

"Yeah, can't blame you for that. Let me transfer your call to Terry Mendez. He might be able to help, but if this is already at the Attorney General's office, this could be above his pay grade."

"Yeah, I can't disagree. I think this is certainly way above my pay grade. If you would transfer me over to Mendez, I'll see what he says."

"Okay, nice to hear your voice, Dev. We're overdue to grab dinner some night."

"I'd love it. Let me get this mess out of my hair, and I'll give you a call."

"Okay. Transferring you now. Don't hang up," Aaron said.

The phone rang twice, and then a man answered, "Mendez."

"Hi, Officer Mendez. My name is Dev Haskell, and I'm a Private Investigator. Aaron LaZelle transferred my call over to you."

"Haskell, I've heard of you."

"Don't believe what you heard. I'm really a nice guy."

Fortunately, he laughed at my comment. "So what can I do for you."

I explained Ernest Stanton's request to look into Gretchen Donahue. I didn't mention Stanton's name.

"Right off the top, my first thought is that this client, or potential client of yours, suspects he's under investigation. If the state is looking into you or your business, they don't do that sort of thing randomly. They would have to have a reasonable suspicion, based on facts. Your suggestion that the individual might just be a potential client they want to check out doesn't really work. An investment firm would request financial information that they would then confirm themselves. If they're in any way successful, they would be doing this numerous times on any given day."

"So why ask me to get involved?"

"That's the ten thousand dollar question. I don't have an answer for you. But it strikes me as very strange and suggests they want information, any and all information, on this individual. I wish I could suggest a more positive situation, but I just can't think of one."

"Well, thank you for your time, and I appreciate your honest appraisal."

"Nice talking to you, Mr. Hassle," Mendez said and disconnected before I could thank him again.

So much for my increasing list of clients. I walked around the block with Morton, and we headed back into the office. Louie was just closing his briefcase. He gave a wave and headed out. I sat at my desk and wondered what I should do.

Eleven

After thinking about calling Tracey to see how she was doing I quickly decided against it. I put Morton in the car, and we drove over to the Midway district. I drove past Percy Riggs' building. His car was parked in the same spot as the last time I saw it. I thought about getting a tracking device and attaching it to his car, but then what? Check him out driving to and from work? It was early in the day, and I made a mental note to come back toward the end of the day and see where he went once he left the office. I spent the rest of the day wasting time in my office. Louie was back after the noon hour. He gave me an update on his morning court appearance and then asked me if everything was okay three or four times over the course of the afternoon.

I took Morton home at 4:30 and got him settled down. I drove over to the Midway district and parked across the street from Percy's building.

I recognized the woman from his office as she stepped out of the building, climbed into a blue Chevy Malibu, and drove out of the parking lot a couple of minutes after 5:30. I waited for Percy to appear. At 7:15,

I unwrapped the last of the three Snickers candy bars I'd bought and ate it in about sixty seconds. Percy eventually stepped out of the building at 8:35. I made a note on the legal pad and followed him at a distance. He pulled into the parking lot at the Kowalski's grocery store on Grand Avenue and was back in his car twelve minutes later with a large grocery bag. I followed him down Grand Avenue. He made a right-hand turn onto Grotto Street, drove past Lincoln Avenue, and down the alley. He pulled into the three-stall garage at 716 Lincoln, where he rented the third-floor apartment. A minute or two after the garage door went down, the lights on the third floor came on.

I felt the odds were slim to none that he had a plan to go anywhere tonight, and since my stomach was growling, I drove over to the nearest McDonald's and got a Big Mac and a chocolate shake. I dined behind the steering wheel of my car and then drove home. Morton was stretched out in the den, gnawing on a chew toy. I turned on the TV, and we watched the evening news, then went upstairs to bed.

We left for the office early the following morning and drove past Percy's building. Since it was just a few minutes after 7:00, I had planned to park and see what time Percy arrived. His car was already in the lot. I parked and waited to see when his employees arrived. His two employees, the man and woman, pulled in about ten minutes apart. The guy at 8:00 and the woman ten minutes later. I walked past their cars. Both vehicles had a child's car seat attached to the backseat. The car seat in the woman's car was pink.

Once in the office, I turned off the coffee pot that had been left on overnight and dumped the remnants down the drain. I let the pot cool for a few minutes, then rinsed it out and made a fresh pot.

Louie arrived just before 9:00. I had a coffee waiting for him, and after he'd recovered from his climb up to the office, he said, "Hi Dev, I didn't expect to see you in here. Weren't you working late last night?"

I went on to tell him about the hours Percy Riggs apparently kept. "So, I drove over to his office this morning, figuring I would park and see when he arrived, and his car was already there. God Bless his soon-to-be ex-wife Tracey, but if he's having an affair with someone, he must be getting up in the middle of the night to do it."

"Sounds like he really is working long hours."

"Yeah, I guess that's the good news. Which reminds me, I haven't heard from her," I said and placed a call.

"Dev?" is how she answered.

"Yeah, Tracey. Just checking in to see how you're doing. You recovered from the other night?"

"Oh, please. I'm so embarrassed. I woke up on the couch in the middle of the night, and I can't remember even eating the pizza. Did we talk?"

"Well, I tried to, but you were more than a little over-served. You were on a phone call when I left," I lied.

"God, that's what I get for drinking a bottle of wine by myself. I'm really sorry. I had such great plans for the night."

I didn't respond to that comment and said, "The pizza was really good, much appreciated. I've been checking out Percy. As far as I can tell, he's working some very long hours. He's in the office before 7:00 and seems to be there all day until late in the evening."

"Does he go anywhere at night?"

"Yeah, back to the place he's renting. He parks in the garage and heads up to his apartment. If anyone was up there waiting for him, they were waiting in the dark."

"What about someone in his office?"

"They appear to be leaving at a somewhat normal time, right around 5:30. They're back around 8:00 in the morning. By the way, both of them have car seats in their cars, so they've got kids they're dealing with, and it's not like there's a private room in the guy's office. It's all one big room."

"So what are you telling me?"

"Nothing, other than I'm still checking Percy out. That's pretty much all I've found out so far. Oh, and he grocery shops at Kowalski's on Grand Avenue."

"Anything else?" she asked, not sounding very happy.

"No, that's what I know thus far. I'll keep checking. Have you had any interaction with that Davy person who came over to our table at Shamrock's the other night?"

"Oh, Davy Ruff? Don't worry about him. He just has to learn that I'm not that interested in him."

"Just be careful. He struck me as the type of person that, regardless of what you do or tell him, he's going to think you need to be with him, and he's liable to do something crazy."

"Oh, he's really not like that. He does some occasional work for me. He's a photographer and very good at that, but he's never really grown socially, if that translates. Other than his mother, I'm probably one of the few women he talks to, and it's all business. If I found out he had Asperger's or something along those lines, it wouldn't surprise me. We met once for lunch to talk over a photo shoot, and I think he was hoping it would be more social. Don't worry about Davy. Just find something on Percy."

"Well, you be careful. I had the distinct feeling he would have inserted himself if you hadn't backed him off. He's liable to get aggressive." I wondered if Davy Ruff had taken the photographs hanging in Tracey's office.

"I don't think he'd do that. I—Oh, I've got to take this call coming in. Chat later," she said and disconnected. Interesting, not a very happy-sounding person, and I couldn't blame it on a hangover from her wine consumption thirty-six hours earlier.

"Everything okay?" Louie asked.

"I'm beginning to think my new clients don't seem to be working out all that well."

"It comes with the business," Louie said.

"Yeah, I guess it does. Well, nothing I can really change. It just strikes me as strange. I must be missing something somewhere. But for the life of me, I can't figure out what it is."

Morton and I went for a walk before I took him home just after 4:00. I drove over to Percy Riggs' office and parked in the back of the parking lot. His female employee left around 5:00, and the guy left twenty minutes later. I stretched out and was prepared to wait with a chocolate shake, three cheeseburgers, and an order of fries from McDonald's.

Apparently, I dozed off for a moment. Fortunately, Percy slamming the driver's door on his Chevy Equinox and turning the car on brought me back to life. I waited until he drove out of the lot before I started my car. As it came to life, the clock on the dashboard registered the time as 9:25. I followed Percy home. Just like the night before, he pulled into the garage, and a minute or two later, the lights came on up on the third floor.

As I headed home, I noticed a pair of headlights behind me. I turned off onto a side street, and sure enough, the vehicle followed maybe a half-block behind me. I drove over to St. Clair Avenue, then took a right onto Pleasant Avenue, drove beneath the 35E bridge onto Victoria, and pulled to the curb four blocks later at The Spot. The same set of headlights was a block and a half behind me. As I got out of my car and headed for the side door in The Spot, the vehicle took the next left. It was a black SUV. I hurried back to my car, made a U-turn, and took the second right. I drove down to the corner, turned right again, and drove two blocks to Randolph Avenue. I pulled up to the intersection and glanced to my right. The black SUV was parked halfway up the block, three doors away from The Spot.

I debated what to do for a moment, then backed up to the alley, drove down another block, and turned onto Randolph Avenue. I was now a block and a half behind the SUV. I waited for a bus to pass, then pulled behind it and drove past the SUV, checking out the license plate number. It was the same bald guy behind the wheel that I'd seen before. The bus pulled to the curb in front of The Spot. I passed it and headed up the street, checking my rearview mirror. The SUV remained parked on the street. I pulled onto a side street and wrote the license plate number on the McDonald's bag. I headed home, checking my rearview mirror a half-dozen times, but never saw the SUV. I parked in my garage, let Morton out the back door, and grabbed a beer from the refrigerator. Morton and I watched the evening news. With the lights off in the house, I looked out the windows but didn't see the SUV, and we headed up to bed.

Twelve

half minute before my alarm went off I crawled out of bed. Morton was still asleep. I pulled on jeans and a t-shirt and drove past Percy's office at 6:45. His car was parked in the same place as yesterday and the day before. I headed home for breakfast. Morton and I were down in the office just a little after 8:00. I made a fresh pot of coffee and, to no avail, scanned the apartment across the street with my binoculars for fifteen minutes. Louie pulled in behind my car a little before 9:00, and I put the binoculars away.

Once he'd recovered from his stair climb, he asked, "So, how'd your night go?"

"Wild and crazy, I sat in my car for about five hours eating cheeseburgers and fries and waiting for Percy Riggs to leave his office. Once he finally left, he went straight home. I drove past his office at 6:45 this morning, and he was already there. I'm quickly coming to the opinion that he's simply a workaholic, and he's not involved in some extramarital affair."

"Sounds boring, but maybe that's good."

"Oh, there was one thing that happened. I followed him home and noticed a black SUV on my tail. I took a couple of different turns, and it was definitely following me. I parked on the side street next to The Spot and got out, making it look like I was heading inside. The SUV went around the block and parked a couple doors down the street from the entrance. I wrote down the guy's license number," I said and held up the McDonald's bag. "I'm going to make a call to my pal over at the DMV in just a bit. Thought it might be nice to let him have a coffee before he had to deal with me."

Louie shook his head and laughed. "Always thinking of other people, Dev."

I called Dave McGovern at the DMV. "McGovern," he answered in his usual way.

"Hi Dave, surprise, surprise. Dev Haskell and I need some info on a license plate."

"Some nice-looking woman who was minding her own business, and you're thinking of ruining her day?"

"Very funny, not. No, I'm being followed, and I don't recognize the vehicle."

"Followed? Seriously? I thought that was what you were paid to do."

"Yeah, so did I, but this guy was definitely following me last night. I took a couple of different turns, and he dropped back but never lost sight of me. I wasn't driving on any streets where I could have cut him off or held him up at a stop light."

"Someone's irate husband?"

"That would be okay. At least it would suggest I was getting some action, but that's not the case, either."

"Better give me the number, and let's see what we come up with." I read the number off to him. "Hmmmm, interesting. Apparently, your man is a competitor."

"What?"

"A black 2020 Chevy Tahoe. It's registered to a guy named Luther Harris at a company called Harris Discovery. You familiar with this guy?"

"No, I don't think I've ever heard of him. You said Harris Discovery?" I asked as I wrote the guy's name, business address, and phone number down on my legal pad.

"Yeah, that's the firm, and the guy's first name is Luther. The company is listed as a private investigation firm."

"Maybe he's new to the biz. That name is just not ringing a bell with me."

"Well, apparently, he's the person who's been driving the SUV around."

"You wouldn't happen to have a photo of the guy, would you?"

"I'm sure you could look him up online, Dev, and get all of that information."

"Okay, sorry to bother you, Dave. Thanks, appreciate the help," I said and disconnected.

I went online and googled the Harris Discovery Agency. There it was, a photo of the same bald guy I'd seen driving the black SUV. I pegged his age around fifty-five or sixty. He was wearing a dark, three-piece suit with a matching tie and a silk pocket cloth, seated at a desk with a large desktop computer screen and some neatly stacked files. Behind him were bookshelves filled with law books. The walls appeared to be paneled. It had been years since I was in an office like that. Nowadays, everything is on the computer. The site listed Harris Discovery with the same downtown address and phone number that Dave McGovern had given me.

"You in court this morning?" I asked Louie.

He shook his head and said, "I've got an appearance at 2:00. I'll be out of here around 1:00. You thinking of going somewhere?"

"Yeah. Does the name Harris Discovery ring a bell with you?"

Louie seemed to think for a minute and then shook his head. "I don't think I've ever heard of them. Is it some kind of tech company?"

"Apparently, the guy is a private investigator. The plate on the SUV that's been following me is registered to that firm, and the guy's name is Luther Harris."

Louie shook his head. "Definitely not ringing a bell."

"Let me take Morton for a walk, and then I'm going to head downtown. The place is located down in the Northern Warehouse building," I said. Louie shook his head in response. I stepped over to the door and grabbed Morton's leash. He hopped off his pillow and hurried next to me with his tail banging against a file cabinet.

"Back in fifteen minutes," I said, and we headed out the door.

As soon as I stepped out of the building, I glanced up and down the street in search of a black Chevy Tahoe. I guess it was a good thing I didn't see one or bald Luther Harris. We took our normal route around the corner and through the neighborhood. The only thing different was we didn't step into The Spot. Morton left his mark on both of his usual fire hydrants, and we were back in the office ten minutes later. I unclipped his leash, tossed him a biscuit, gave Louie a wave, and went out to my car.

I waited for a truck to pass, then made a U-turn and headed down Randolph Avenue to West Seventh Street. I took a left at the intersection and headed downtown. I turned right onto Kellogg Boulevard and took another right onto Broadway, just past the Union Depot. I parked in the Farmers Market lot since there wasn't a market today and went across the street to the Northern Warehouse building.

The building is a massive six-story red brick building built back in 1908. The solid building looks like the walls would be about six feet thick. It housed a bar that was closed and some offices on the first floor, but the building is actually known for its artist lofts. I walked into the main entrance and back to the bank of elevators. Harris Discovery was listed in unit 605. I took the elevator up to the sixth floor and walked down the hallway past number 605 to the end of the hall. I found it interesting that, at least on the sixth floor, all the units appeared to be occupied. The names were unique, everything from Impressionist Dempsey to Starlight Creations, and in a couple of areas, there was the slightest scent of turpentine. I walked back down the hall to unit 605, Harris Discovery. I paused for a second and then stepped into the office.

Based on the photo I'd seen online, I expected a receptionist behind a counter and maybe a couch and a coffee table with outdated magazines. Instead, I stepped into a very small office, about one-third the size of my office. It was barely large enough for Luther Harris and the card table that served as his desk. The large desk, along with the desktop computer screen, the bookcase with the law books, and the wood-paneled walls, were gone. The walls were sheet-rocked and taped but not painted. Harris had two metal folding chairs set in front of his desk. The chairs were stenciled 'ASSUMPTION CHURCH' on the back in black spray paint. They were obviously stolen from the downtown church. An empty pizza box rested on one of the folding chairs.

Bald, wide-eyed, Luther Harris sat staring from behind his card table, wearing a Minnesota Twins t-shirt, and he was in need of a shave. "Now, hold on just a moment. You're Haskell, right? It's a free country, and I haven't done anything to you."

"You know who I am?"

"I just told you. You're that Haskell guy. A PI."

"Yeah, and you're Luther Harris, the guy who's been following me in a black Chevy Tahoe."

"Like I said, it's a free country. Besides, I, I don't even know what you're talking about."

"Come on, man. You followed me last night. You parked a couple of doors down from The Spot bar. What time did you finally go home?"

"It was late," he said, then shook his head and said, "Anyway, that wasn't me."

I shook my head and said, "Mind if I sit down in one of these chairs you stole from Assumption Church? You know, they're clients of mine." I lied as I pulled a chair back and settled in across from Harris.

"I didn't steal them. I just borrowed them for a bit. So, what do you want anyway?"

I thought for a moment, then said, "Just wondering why you're following me."

"I'm not following you. I don't even know who you are."

"Luther, you already said my name, and you know I'm a P.I. I got your license plate number. You're driving a 2020 black Chevy Tahoe. Your car is registered to your firm. You followed me down to The Spot bar last night. Why don't you tell me what you're looking for, and maybe I can help you out and save us both a lot of time and headache?"

"I got nothing to say."

I thought for a minute and said, "Does this have anything to do with an investment guy named Ernest Stanton?"

He got a puzzled look on his face and said, "Who is that?"

The look on his face suggested he had no idea who Stanton was, which left only one other name. Tracey Wilde. If it had something to do with Tracey, the most likely person to hire Luther Harris was probably Percy Riggs. I could only hope Percy was getting a good deal.

"How about this, Luther? Can I buy you lunch?" Amazingly, he agreed.

Thirteen

The Black Dog bar used to be on the ground floor of the building, but after two decades in business, they'd closed last year, so we walked a block up the street to the Burrito Red Mexican Grill. The bar was half-full, and we settled in at a table in the corner of the dining area. Harris ordered two fried chicken burritos and a Coke. I'd never been to the place before, so I ordered the same thing.

We chatted about nothing in particular until our meals and the two cokes arrived, and then I asked, "How long have you been working as a PI, Luther? I checked out your website. I have to tell you, it was really nice. Where was that photo taken? Did you move offices?"

He shook his head and said, "I'm just getting into this gig. I worked for a collection agency for twenty years. Owned by a friend I'd known since we were kids. He died last year from cancer."

"Oh, sorry, I've been through that. Never any fun losing a friend."

"Yeah, you're telling me. His son took over the business, knew nothing about it, and started making all kinds of changes. He brought in some younger folks. It became pretty obvious I was on the way out whether I wanted to be or not. So I gave my notice, got my PI license, and started from scratch. In a way, I'm dealing with the same strata of the population."

"But the image on your website, the fancy desk, that large computer screen, the shelves of law books behind you. The walls were paneled. You're wearing a suit and tie. For God's sake, you really looked, I don't know, successful."

"Yeah, well, that's thanks to my one and only client. He loaned me the suit coat. I had the shirt and tie. Everything else in that image came off of a computer. The desk, the law books, and even the stack of files were all added to my image. I got a bucket of painted rocks a neighborhood kid did for me, and I told the landlords I was an artist and showed them the rocks. That's how I got this space in the Artist Collective."

I was starting to like this guy. "So let me make a guess here. Based on what you're telling me about your one and only client being a computer guy. His name wouldn't happen to be Percy Riggs, and his business is Technical Percy. Does that sound right?"

Harris took another bite of his burrito and nodded. "Yeah, I have no idea how in the hell he found my name. I'm just glad he did."

"And he gave you my name to check out."

He nodded and took another bite. "Don't take it the wrong way. You seem like a nice enough guy. Besides, you're buying me lunch. You know how it goes. I need the business."

"Yeah, preaching to the choir on that level. Well, what does he want you to find out?"

He seemed to think about that for a long moment, then said, "He wants to know who you're working for and what they want. He's worried it might be a potential client. You actually stopped in at his office, didn't you? Checking things out?"

"He knew that was me?"

"Well, if you took a few seconds to look at his office, you'd know right away he's a tech guy. He showed me an image of you standing just inside the door. You said you were looking for a friend and gave a name, which I've already forgotten."

"I asked for my friend Kevin O'Brien. God bless him. He was a great guy who passed away a few years ago. But back up, you said he had a picture of me."

"Actually, a recording from the moment you stepped into the place until you left. I don't think it's even a minute long, but yeah, it was you."

"But I never told him my name. It's not like he could look out a window and get my license number. There aren't any windows in that office. In fact, I'm trying to recall, but I don't think there are any windows in that building."

"Yeah, that's right. I think that was one of his requirements for his office location. Like I said, he's a tech guy. He's got some facial recognition programs. God, he's such a genius he probably developed the programs himself. Anyway, he ran your image through facial recognition, and your name came up. Your office is just across the street from that bar you go to every day, don't you?"

"You mean The Spot. Yeah, it's a nice place. You should check it out sometime."

"So, who are you working for?"

"Believe me, not a potential client. Someone who is in the process of not interacting with him at all."

He thought about that. "Haskell, you're working for his soon-to-be ex-wife, aren't you." I just shrugged. "You know the deal there? What she does?"

"Yeah, she's a fashion model or something. She's always working on photo shoots. In fact, we went to dinner one night, and some whacko guy who takes her pictures came over to our table. Threatened me when I asked him to leave. She told me later he was a photographer she uses from time to time and that he has issues. I was ready to punch him right where he was standing, but she got him to leave. I don't think I've seen the guy since. As a matter of fact, when I first spotted your car, I thought you might be him. Fortunately, you weren't. He struck me as just crazy enough to do something really stupid."

"Interesting story. I like that you think she's a fashion model."

"Oh, she is. I was in her house a couple of nights
ago, and there were photos of her and a large impression-
istic painting of her hanging over her fireplace. By the
way, nothing happened. I had some pizza, and she ended
up on a phone call, and I went home. End of story."

He stabbed what was left of his burrito with a fork,
shoved it into his mouth, and said, "Mmm-mmm, I'd
love to see the pictures of her. Haskell, she's not a fashion model. Tracey Wilde is a porn star. Her stage name
is Racey Tracey."

I almost choked on the burrito in my mouth. I
coughed a couple of times and then grabbed my glass of
coke and took a couple of hefty swallows. That only
seemed to make things worse. I coughed, felt my eyes
water, and, after a minute or two, gradually regained
control. "Tracey is a porn star?"

"Yeah. How could you not know that?"

"Honest, I had no idea. God, are you sure? I mean—
umm, okay, first of all. You can tell your client, Percy,
that I have been above board the entire time. Strictly professional. There has been no sex with her. When we had
dinner that time, it was at Shamrock's on West Seventh
Street. Lots of people in the place, and we sat on opposite
sides of the booth. The one time I was at her house over
in Mendota, she'd just finished up a photo shoot and, I
guess, was celebrating. It probably was porn, but I had
no idea. She had a little too much wine, and she passed

out while she was on the phone. I grabbed a slice or two of pizza and left."

"So you don't know about her tattoo."

"You mean her 'Please, Sir' tattoo? Yeah, I do know about it, but only because I was in her office, and I saw it in a picture. Oh, and it's in the painting of her hanging over the fireplace. I thought it was a fake thing. You know a joke," I said. I didn't want to admit that I had been studying her very perfect ass in the tight white shorts when she led me into the kitchen. "How long has she been doing that, anyway? Was she in porn when they were married?"

Luther nodded. "Yes, but it's only been recently that her career, if you can call it that, has taken off. She's not stupid, and apparently, in that business, you've maybe got a year or two to take it to the bank, and then you're either exhausted, replaced, you've gone crazy, or all of the above. She initially was some kind of a model but somehow got into the porn biz and kept it quiet. When Percy found out, he gave her the option of either quitting or he was going to leave. Now you know which one she chose."

I shook my head. "It's not that I don't believe you. It's just that I had absolutely no idea. But now that I think about it, yeah, it explains the half-dozen framed photos in her office."

"And maybe the guy who interrupted your dinner."

I nodded and then just shook my head.

Fourteen

A quick look at the bill, I paid, and we walked back toward Harris's office in the Artist Collective. "So Luther, does your investigation of me have an end date?" I asked.

"Not really. Percy just wants me to find out anything and everything I can about you. Unfortunately for me, you're almost as boring as I am."

I laughed at that. "I tell you what, at the end of the day, I usually join my office mate, Louie Laufen, over at The Spot. Why don't you join us? I can tell you some of the things I'm involved in. Nothing really interesting, but at least it will look like you're doing your homework. Then, if you have any information on Percy, maybe you'd want to share it."

"I can tell you what I know about Percy. He's focused on that business. He's in there from early morning till late at night. When he's finished for the day, he goes home, has dinner, and goes to bed. He's even more boring than me."

"Well, please join us tonight. We're usually in there by 5:30. My pal Louie is a rather large guy. He sits on

the same stool at the far end of the bar and drinks bourbon."

Luther nodded and said, "I really appreciate that. It
will make me look good. I'll be there on one condition."
I was afraid he was going to say, 'Don't ask me about
Percy.' Instead, he said, "I get to buy you both a drink."

"Sounds like a deal to me," I said, and we shook
hands. Luther headed into the Artist Collective building,
and I walked over to my car in the Farmers Market lot.
It was a little after 1:00 when I got back to the office.
Louie was gone, and Morton was half-asleep. As I
stepped into the office, Morton opened one eye. As soon
as he saw it was me, he closed his eye, snuggled into his
pillow, and took a deep breath.

I poured myself a coffee, turned on my computer,
and Googled the name, Racey Tracey. A site came up
requiring me to click on a box that stated I was over
twenty-one years of age. Of course, I clicked on the box.
A half-dozen thirty-minute videos appeared offering a
free three-minute intro, and then, if I paid the price, I
could download the videos for $9.99 each. I decided to
investigate the first video, Racey Tracey Bare, produced
by a company called Bad Girl Lovers, Inc.

Louie stepped back into the office right around 3:00.
I had just finished watching the third video and was in
the process of buying the fourth. He gave me a wave and
settled into his chair. Fortunately, I was wearing headphones, so he couldn't hear the moaning and the exple-
tives being shouted. He glanced over at me three or four

times before he finally got up and filled his coffee mug. Halfway through the fourth video, I paused the screen and pulled off my headphones.

"What are you listening to?" Louie asked as he leaned back in his chair.

"Oh, some video from a client. Part of my investigation into Percy Riggs."

"Finding anything interesting?"

I nodded. "Yeah," I said and headed in a different direction. "But get this, I was able to meet up with a guy earlier. Remember I mentioned the black SUV I thought had been following me and that it was owned by a private investigator?"

"Yeah, I remember. Can't recall what the guy's name was."

"Luther Harris, his firm is called Harris Discovery. I paid him a visit. I drove down to his office and knocked on the door. We ended up grabbing lunch, and I asked him to join us at The Spot tonight."

"He's investigating you, and you asked him to join us?"

"Yeah. Relax, he's a nice guy, and I actually like him. He's just starting out. It just so happens that Percy Riggs hired him to investigate me. We had a nice talk over lunch. He gave me some information on my client, Tracey Wilde."

"Was it useful information?"

"Just your basic background stuff, but still nice to know and interesting. Anyway, that's been my day. Things go well for you in court?"

"I don't know if 'well' is the word I'd use. But to no surprise, my client was arrested for driving under the influence. It was a second-degree DWI. Can you think of a better time to suggest that the arresting officer was abusing her rights? She accused him of sexual misconduct when he asked her to take the breathalyzer test. Of course, since she refused to take the test, the policy is that he hauls her downtown. That led to her ranting and raving in the back of the squad car for the next ten minutes during the drive down to the station. Unfortunately, it's all recorded on his body cam, which was played in court. Not her first offense. She's got two priors, so she's the proud owner of a suspended license and will be considering her next move over the course of the next six months while waiting in jail. Oh, and then there's the three thousand dollar fine."

"She's locked up for six months?"

"That's what happens when you tell the judge he doesn't have a right to sentence you, and then you call him some rather colorful names."

"Sounds like she's going to lose her job."

"Not a problem. She's a trust fund baby. Hasn't worked a day in her life."

"Hopefully, that means you'll get paid, eventually."

Louie shook his head. "I've dealt with her before, so I've been paid in advance."

Louie headed over to The Spot, and I took Morton for a walk. As we approached The Spot toward the end of our walk, I noticed the black 2020 Chevy Tahoe parked next to the building. When we entered the bar, Louie was seated on his usual stool at the end of the bar. Just now, he appeared to be laughing at something Luther Harris had told him. Luther was seated on the stool next to Louie.

"Get you a beer?" Mike asked as we stepped inside.

"Hi, Mike. Yeah, thanks. Better pour Louie another and get whatever the guy next to him is drinking.

We headed down the bar. Morton strained on his leash, pulling me all the way. As soon as we rounded the corner, Louie bent down with his handful of pork rinds.

"Oh, so Louie has been telling me this is your better half, Dev. Nice to meet you, Malcom," Luther said.

"His name is Morton, and yeah, he's a lot nicer than me on a number of levels."

"You take him for a walk before you come in here?" Luther asked.

"Yeah, it's better for all involved, including Morton. Have you been here long?"

Luther shook his head. "I pulled up just as Louie was stepping in the front door. Nice neighborhood place. I've never been in here before," he said and glanced around. There were about fifteen other people in the place at the moment, but it was early.

"He was telling me you two are investigating each other," Louie said.

I shook my head and went on to explain things, which led to Luther giving us the lowdown on Percy Riggs. Basically, he was a guy who worked seven days a week, building his business. He was smart, bordering on genius, in Luther's mind. I explained that his soon-to-be former wife was convinced he was having an affair with another woman or a number of women.

Luther shook his head. "Based on her business, that's not surprising. Like I told you, he's working seven days a week. I've met him at his office a number of times. He's always there, all day, every day. The woman who works for him has two little kids, and even if she wanted to fool around, which she doesn't, she hasn't got the time. The guy who works for him is finishing up a doctorate in some version of computer science. Percy told me what it was, and just the name was over my head. Percy is a nice guy. How he ever got married to Tracey is beyond me."

"Do you know, is he paying her anything?" I asked.

Luther shook his head. "Not that I'm aware of. To be honest, up until a few months ago, she was making more money than Percy. He's in the process of landing a big tech company as a client. It's not Amazon, but it's like they were twenty-five years ago. That's why he's putting in all the hours. I don't know this for certain, but I'm sure Tracey is unaware of his pending success. You certainly wouldn't be able to pick up on it based on his lifestyle. He's a really nice guy who just works all the time. Which makes him a really nice, boring guy. Did you check out any of Tracey's work?"

Even though I paid for the privilege and had spent the better part of three hours of my life watching some of her videos this afternoon, I shook my head. "No, I was going through some other stuff," I said, hoping Louie didn't pick up on what I'd been watching.

"The little I've seen were very good. There was this one scene—"

Fortunately, Mike arrived with a fresh drink for Louie, another beer for Luther, and my first beer. We all raised a glass to Mike, toasted him, and took a sip. "What do you have lined up for future work?" I asked Luther, hopefully changing the subject.

He shook his head. "Like everyone who's self-employed, it's feast or famine. I've done a couple of very tiny projects, but like I said earlier today, checking you out, Dev, is the first real investigation I've had that lasted more than a couple of hours. Now, after our conversations, Percy is probably going to tell me he's heard enough. I thought the night you were over at her house was going to lead to a lot more investigation. Then when you pulled out of there ninety minutes later, well, let's just say I was disappointed."

"I didn't know you were even there. You didn't mention it over lunch."

"I was just being cautious. She's busy all day, every day, too. It's just that it's a different business. You mentioned that Davy Ruff character. He's over at her place occasionally, but there's always a couple of other folks there at the same time, so I'm pretty sure that's strictly business. Did I mention Ruff has whiskey plates on his car?"

"No, you didn't. What kind of car does he drive? I'd like to make sure he's not following me around."

"It's a pea-green Chevy Spark. I think a 2015. I got the plate number written down somewhere. Whiskey plates, you know what they look like?"

"I do. They're white with a six-digit plate number that begins with the letter 'W,'" I said. We chatted on for another hour and had two more beers. Luther Harris eventually left, and Morton and I took off five minutes later.

Fifteen

Despite what Luther Harris told me the night before, I set the alarm for an hour earlier and went to bed after the evening news. I was sound asleep when the alarm went off at 5:45. Morton didn't move. I got dressed and headed downstairs. I filled a travel mug with coffee and headed over to the Midway district and the Technical Percy office. I was approaching the parking lot in front of the building just as the driver's door opened on the only car in the lot, Percy's white Chevy Equinox. Apparently, he'd just pulled into the lot.

I continued down the street and checked the clock on my dashboard, 6:12 AM. I just shook my head. The guy was working fourteen and fifteen-hour days. No wonder he wasn't dating anyone. If I hung around his house after following him home, there was probably a pretty good chance he was in bed within thirty minutes.

I headed home, grabbed a shower, and was in the kitchen for almost an hour before Morton wandered downstairs. I gave him his head scratch. He stretched as I opened the back door and then headed outside. I filled his food and water dishes, and once he finished breakfast, we hopped in the car and drove down to the office.

Louie showed up just before 9:00. I watched as he parked his Ford Fiesta behind my car. I dumped yesterday's coffee remnants from his mug into the sink and refilled his mug. "Fresh coffee on the picnic table for you," I said once he entered the office. He settled into his chair, and after a few minutes, he said, "Thanks. Did you go home after The Spot?"

"Yeah, I made an early morning check on Percy Riggs. I drove over to his building, expecting him to eventually show up. He was just getting out of his car and heading into the building. That was at 6:12 this morning, and I'll check tonight, but odds are he'll be there until 8:30 or 9:00. Like Luther said last night, the guy puts in incredible hours seven days a week. Nothing short of amazing."

"You just hope it works for him," Louie said.

I got online, and despite wanting to watch another Racey Tracey video, I began searching the internet for anything on Gretchen Donahue, the investigator for the Attorney General's office that Ernest Stanton had me looking into. At no surprise, I wasn't able to find much. I shut down my computer and grabbed the leash. Morton jumped to his feet and stood at the door with his tail wagging.

"You guys going for a walk?" Louie asked without looking away from his computer screen.

"We're going to check something out. Hopefully, it won't take more than an hour. You going anywhere?" I asked.

Louie shook his head. "I'm glued to my computer for the rest of the day."

"See you in a while," I said, and we headed out to the car. I put Morton in the backseat, and we headed up Randolph Avenue for a couple of miles. I drove past Saint Catherine University, formerly College of St. Catherine, and took a right turn onto Cleveland Avenue. I took the next left onto West James Avenue, the street Gretchen Donahue lived on. I pulled to the curb a block before her house, I got Morton out of the backseat, and we walked down past the Donahue house. As we passed her place, a little dog in the house began barking.

Morton's tail began to wag, and I spotted a Miniature Schnauzer in what looked like Gretchen Donahue's living room. The dog was standing on a couch, looking out the front window and barking. Morton gave a couple of friendly barks in return.

We continued down the street and walked up the alley past her garage, with the high fence and an apple tree in the backyard. On a whim, we circled the block and walked past again. Just as we approached the house, the front door opened, and a woman who appeared similar to the online photo I'd seen of Gretchen Donahue stepped out of the house with the Miniature Schnauzer on a leash. Both dogs immediately strained on their leashes and barked at one another. Not a vicious bark, but more like saying, 'Hey, it's nice to meet you.'

"No, Timmy, now that's enough. Oh, sorry, he was barking up a storm a few minutes ago, and I thought I'd better take him for a walk before I went to work. Sorry to cause an uproar," Donahue said and laughed as they headed toward Morton and me.

"Oh, not a problem. As a matter of fact, we were probably who he was barking at a few minutes ago. This is Morton, and he spotted your dog standing on the couch, and so he barked, which got both of them going. We went around the block, and he insisted on going past your house again. Sorry if we caused a problem. They just sounded so glad to see one another."

She laughed at that and said, "I can't blame him. I'm gone all day, so any interaction is a big deal. Oh, by the way, my name is Gretchen."

"Nice to meet you, Gretchen. You too, Timmy. My name is Dev, and this is Morton."

"Do you live nearby?" she asked. At the moment, Morton and Timmy appeared to be in the process of becoming fast friends.

"No, we're just here for a walk. We walked over on the campus and around the pond," I lied. "Morton seemed to still have some energy, so we walked through the neighborhood. You live in a lovely area."

"Oh, thank you. Yes, I've been here for a number of years. Do you live in town?"

"Yeah, we're down by the Cathedral. I was on my way to the office, and Mr. Energy seemed to need a walk. It's such a lovely morning, we just kept going. Would you care to join us? There's nowhere in particular we're headed."

"We always go down to the River Boulevard. There's a path there and plenty of room."

"May we join you?" I asked.

"I think we would both like that."

"You lead the way, and we'll follow," I said.

We crossed Cretin Avenue and took a right down Randolph. The River Boulevard and the path were just two blocks ahead. Along the way, we chatted about the weather, dogs, the city, and more dogs. We crossed the winding River Boulevard road. One side was covered with large homes that some would call mansions. The opposite side of the boulevard ran along the Mississippi River bluff for four or five miles. It overlooked the river and the wooded park below. We stepped onto the paved path and headed downriver. Every so often, we passed a bench overlooking the river below.

It wasn't crowded, but we passed the occasional walker and three or four joggers. We chatted along the way. Gretchen told me she worked for the state. I told her I was self-employed. Morton and Timmy seemed to get along wonderfully.

After about a half mile, we approached a scenic overlook with a circular drive, a small parking lot, and a contemporary stone sculpture. Gretchen said, "Well, this is where we usually turn back. Unfortunately, I have to get to work."

"Yeah, I should do the same. It's been wonderful to meet you. Timmy made Morton's day. Once we get down to the office, I suspect he'll be asleep within ten minutes."

"Wouldn't that be nice? You go for a walk and then come home and take a nap."

"Don't tempt me," I said.

"Oh, believe me. I deal with people doing bad things all day long. It's amazing."

"Same with me, or they're hoping I can somehow clean up a mess. It gets exhausting, and nowadays, attempting to relax while I watch the news is, well, let's just say there is nothing relaxing on the news."

"Amen to that," she said. As we approached her house, I was hoping she might ask me in for a coffee, but instead, she smiled and said, "It was nice to meet you. Hope you have a pleasant day."

"Thanks, Gretchen. Very nice to meet you and thank you for the introduction to the path along the boulevard. We may take that again."

"Yes, it's lovely. Enjoy your day. Come on, Timmy, inside," she said and then had to yank on his leash a couple of times to get him headed for the house. Morton barked a 'Goodbye.' We got a wave from Gretchen after she unlocked the front door. Once they stepped inside, Timmy was on the couch barking. Morton gave a friendly reply, and we headed up the street to the car.

As we drove back to the office, I thought about our meeting. Just the luck of the draw. I met her and knew the name of her dog. She enjoyed playing bridge and traveling and wasn't going to willingly share information on whatever she was working on. It was after 10:00, and she was just heading to work, which suggested to me that she could set her own hours. She wasn't in a nine-to-five office, and she probably worked a lot of evenings and weekends, depending on whatever case she was dealing with.

Louie was on his computer when we stepped into the office. I unclipped Morton's leash, tossed him a biscuit, and he headed for his pillow. The almost empty coffee pot was still on the hot burner, and I turned it off.

"How'd things go?" he asked and continued typing.

"Better than expected," I said as I pulled on my headphones and turned on my computer. I still had one more video to watch, Racey Tracey Plus Two. Once again, the video was produced by Bad Girl Lovers, Inc.

Sixteen

It was close to 1:00. Louie was focused on his computer, and Morton was still asleep. "I'm thinking about heading up to Roosters and grabbing a BBQ sandwich. You interested in some lunch?"

"Yeah, you need some cash?"

"Thanks, but I'm good. Back in fifteen minutes," I said and headed out the door. It's just a two-block walk up the street, and I needed a break. I waited for a bus to pass and then crossed the street and walked up the block. I stepped across the side street. Roosters was at the far end of the block. There was a large white pickup truck parked at the curb with the words Rainbow Tree Service on the passenger door. What caught my attention was the side view mirror on the passenger door with the reflection of what looked like an ugly pea-green Chevy Spark. I remembered Luther mentioning Davy Ruff driving a Chevy Spark. There wasn't any traffic on the street at the moment, and the Spark just seemed to be stopped in the street, waiting.

The entrance to Roosters was three doors away and other than the pickup, there was nothing to hide behind.

I stopped alongside the pickup and pretended to study the door. The Spark remained still for a few seconds until a car approached from behind. It finally accelerated and headed up the street. As it drove past me, standing alongside the truck, it picked up speed. I spotted the white license plate beginning with the letter 'W.' I repeated the plate number and hurried into Roosters.

There were four people in line ahead of me. I stepped to the front of the line, reached across the blonde woman at the head of the line, and grabbed a pen from the coffee mug next to the cash register.

"Umm, excuse me," the blonde woman said.

I pulled out last night's receipt from The Spot and wrote down the whiskey license plate number, then said, "Oh, sorry, I had to write something down before I forgot it."

She looked at me, shook her head, and said, "Scary."

I moved to the back of the line. When I stepped out of Roosters, I glanced up and down the street. Fortunately, I didn't see anything resembling the ugly pea-green Chevy Spark. Still, just to play it safe, I walked behind Roosters and headed back down the alley, almost but not quite running, and all the while looking over my shoulder. I figured the odds of there being more than two incredibly ugly cars like that in the entire metro area was about half of a percent. The odds of one of those cars having whiskey plates and not belonging to Davy Ruff were zero. Totally impossible.

"Oh wow, that didn't take long. Didn't expect you back this fast," Louie said as he pushed his chair back from his desktop computer and slid over to the BBQ sandwich I had just set on his picnic table.

"I was just hungry and wanted to get back and eat."

Morton jumped off his pillow and hurried over with his tail wagging.

Louie studied me for a moment and said, "Everything okay?"

"Yeah, at least it is now that I can sit down and eat." I sat down and unwrapped the BBQ pork sandwich. After a couple of bites, I began to settle down.

"Mmm-mm, good," Louie said. "You know, this is the first time in a long time you didn't bring back one of those beef bones for Morton."

"Oh, yeah, guess I was in such a hurry that I just forgot," I said, then kicked myself.

I placed a call to Luther Harris and ended up leaving a message. "Hi, Luther, Dev Haskell. Hey, give me a call when you have a chance. Thanks." I went online and began searching for information on Davy Ruff. He was listed as president of a company called Fantasy Foxxx. Beyond that, there was no information on the company, no website, not so much as an address or a phone number available, let alone a sample of pictures. But then, if the only pictures he was taking were of Tracey in her work environment, maybe that was wise unless he had them for sale.

Louie headed over to The Spot just after 5:00. I stayed in the office for another ten minutes watching out the window for the pea-green Chevy Spark, but I never saw it. I clipped the leash onto Morton, and we headed out for our walk. I glanced over my shoulder about every forty-five seconds but never saw Ruff or his ugly car. We headed into The Spot through the side door for a change. When we stepped inside, we were right behind Louie, sitting on his stool. Morton stood on his hind legs and placed his paws on Louie's thigh, almost but not quite, causing Louie to spill his drink.

"Oh, well, Morton. I've been expecting you. I just didn't expect you to sneak up from behind." He opened up the bag of pork rinds waiting on the bar and poured a handful out of the bag.

Morton immediately devoured them, then settled back down on the floor and assumed his standard sitting position with a pleading look on his face.

"How did your day go?" Louie asked.

"A little eventful," I replied and went on to tell Louie about spotting Davy Ruff's car on my walk while heading up to Roosters for our sandwiches.

"You think it was just coincidental, and maybe he only happened to be driving by?"

I shook my head. "Not when he came to a stop in the middle of the street and stayed there watching me until a car came up behind him."

"What are you going to do?"

"Nothing, really. I'll give Luther Harris another call and see if he has any ideas. He's got a little more info on the guy than I do."

"You thinking about calling Tracey?"

"I'd prefer not to, just from a business standpoint. Which reminds me, I should only stay for one and then head over to Percy's office and see what time he leaves tonight."

"Well, if he's leaving around 9:00, you got plenty of time."

"Yeah, but I just need to be sure." I had Morton in the car fifteen minutes later, and we headed home. Once I got him settled in, I grabbed a container of Thai stir-fry from the refrigerator and headed over to Percy's office. I parked across the street in a parking lot with a number of other cars and had been eating my stir-fry and waiting for Percy to leave when the pea-green Chevy Spark pulled into the lot. It drove past Percy's car, circled around, and drove past again just as some guy walked out of the building and headed toward a pickup truck. The Chevy Spark exited the lot and disappeared down the street.

I thought about following and then came up with a better idea. I phoned Luther Harris. He answered on the second ring. "Harris."

"Hi, Luther, Dev Haskell."

"Hi, Dev. Got your message and meant to call. Are you taking it easy over at The Spot? Oh, thanks for last night, by the way. Very nice. Great to get to know you better and meet Louie."

"Thanks, Luther, say, I think I've got something for you." I went on to tell him about the pea-green Chevy Spark checking out Percy's car. "My thought is, why don't you come over and just wait in the lot until Percy comes out to leave? Tell him you saw Ruff checking out his car. It might work for a longer gig instead of him ending it when you tell him what a wonderful guy I am."

"Are you over there now?"

"Yeah, actually I'm in the parking lot across the street. Maybe pull in near Percy's car, and we can touch base once you talk to him and he heads home. I don't know what Ruff had in mind if anything. But I'd be careful. He strikes me as someone with issues. If Tracey even casually mentioned something to Ruff, he could take it wrong, and suddenly, he's on a mission from above to take Percy out of the picture."

"I'll be there in fifteen minutes," Harris said and disconnected.

He lied. He was there in eleven minutes. It was toward the end of rush hour, but traffic would still be heavy. He must have run a couple of red lights and gone about sixty miles per hour up University Avenue. He pulled to a stop about fifteen feet behind Percy's Chevy Equinox and pumped his brake lights. A moment later, my phone rang. Luther Harris.

"Hey, Luther, I'm just across the street from you."

"Flash your lights for me." I did that, and he said, "I see you. So you said this Davy Ruff character drove past checking out Percy's car?"

"Yeah, he did a U-turn at the other end of the lot and drove past the car again just as a guy came out of the building, and Ruff took off. I don't know this, but it wouldn't surprise me if he was planning to slit a tire or pour something into the gas tank. Based on what I've seen, Percy's car could be here for another couple hours. That's why I thought, if you hung around, when he finally comes out, you can fill him in, and he's probably going to want to keep you on the payroll. This Davy guy seems to have a pounding heart for Tracey. Although the couple of times she's mentioned him to me, she never suggested anything similar."

"I think the mistake she made was paying him with some, umm, personal attention instead of cash. At least, that's what Percy thinks. Davy Ruff has been a pain for Percy since before he and Tracey separated."

I went on to tell him about Davy Ruff checking me out on my way to Roosters.

"He just stopped in the middle of the street?"

"Yeah, I didn't let on that I saw him, but I stayed alongside a pickup truck until he left. I didn't know if he had a gun or was going to try to run me over. You know, I'm thinking it might not be a bad idea to mention this to Tracey. If the guy is checking out Percy and me, it's not that far-fetched that he might grab Tracey just to keep her safe."

"That would be interesting. Well, I'm going to stay here until Percy comes out. I'm not going to mention your name. I appreciate you giving me the heads-up. Take off if you want. I'm on this."

"Oh, thanks. I think I'll just hang out for a while. Call me after Percy leaves," I said and disconnected. I debated driving over to the gas station and getting a couple of candy bars but decided against it just in case idiot Davy Ruff reappeared. Percy finally stepped out of the building just a little before 9:00.

Seventeen

As soon as Percy stepped outside, Luther hopped out of his car and apparently called his name. Percy looked over, gave a wave, and they met just behind Percy's white Chevy. They talked for a good five minutes. They walked around Percy's car, checking all four tires, and then Luther got down and checked underneath the car.

Percy nodded a number of times, shook Luther's hand, and climbed into his car. After he backed up, he tooted his horn, gave a wave to Luther, and drove off. Luther called me a half-minute later.

"Hey, it looked like that went pretty well," I said.

"Oh, Dev, thank you so much for making me aware of this. He's putting me on the payroll until the divorce goes through, and then he's going to find work for me after that. This is just great. Thanks so much."

"Glad to help, man. We all need it."

"Hey, it's just about 9:00. Would you have time to let me buy you a beer down at The Spot?"

I thought about that for half a second and then said, "Yeah. Tell you what, I'll meet you down there."

"See you there," Luther said. His headlights suddenly came on, and he pulled out of the parking lot. I followed him down to The Spot. He pulled into the place where I usually park. I pulled into the small back lot and parked behind The Spot, just in case Davy Ruff drove past looking for my car. I looked around before I stepped into the bar. Fortunately, everything seemed okay. Two beers were already waiting at the bar. Luther was sitting on the stool next to Louie's, and since Louie wasn't there, I grabbed his stool.

"Here's to you, Dev," Luther said as we raised our beer mugs. We clinked them together, smiled, and took a sip. It was a vast improvement from the bottle of water I drank to wash down the stir-fry.

"Thanks, Luther. I'm just glad that idiot Ruff didn't do something to Percy's car or, worse, do something to Percy."

"Yeah, that guy is a real piece of work."

"Do you know where he lives?"

"No, but I'm willing to guess that Percy does. As you're asking that, I'm thinking it might make sense to check him out. Maybe keep a bit of an eye on the guy."

"If you get his address, pass it on to me. Thank God he drives one of the world's ugliest cars. If he drove some nondescript thing, I probably never would have noticed him and certainly wouldn't have picked up on him checking out Percy's car in the parking lot. Good move, by the way, walking around the car and looking underneath."

"Just a gentle reminder to Percy about how crazy this guy could be. It's interesting. Tracey is one of the best-looking women I've ever seen. There's probably nothing she hasn't done sexually, and Percy can't wait to get away from her."

"You said you don't think he's paying her anything, no support, nothing like that."

Luther shook his head. "No, it's like I told you. Up until six months ago, he wasn't making any money. I'm sure he drained whatever he had in his bank account. Tracey's business was booming. You've been at her place out in Mendota, a lovely unit. She's on that pond, and she's got her own company with some big investor begging to put more money into it. It's kind of sad when you think about it. Suddenly, they're both financially successful, and they can't wait to get a divorce."

"What's holding it up?" I asked.

Luther gave a little shrug. "I think they're just going through the motions. My sense is they've mutually agreed to everything. Now it's just working its way through the court system. Probably a couple of weeks or maybe a month, and it's done."

"You think Percy might ask for some money based on this Ruff character checking him out?"

"What's he going to do? No proof, no pictures. Even if there was a photo, big deal, the guy made a U-turn in a parking lot. Nothing wrong with that. No, I think they both just want to part ways, and the further away from each other they get, the safer Percy will be."

Luther paid for a round, I bought a round, and then it was time to head home. Apparently, a force of habit, but I kept checking my rearview mirror on the way home. Thankfully, I never spotted anyone following me. I pulled into my garage, double-checked the side garage door to make sure it was locked and headed into the house. It was just after 10:30. Morton was already upstairs asleep. I got the coffee ready for the morning, turned off the lights, and went upstairs. I adjusted my alarm back to the normal wake-up time. Once in bed, I was asleep in a couple of minutes.

I was up before my alarm, turned it off, and grabbed a shower. I'd finished breakfast and was on my laptop checking out Tracey when Morton came downstairs. I let him outside and went back to my computer. Tracey had a new video out, apparently released sometime last night. Racey Tracey All Aboard. Once again, the video was produced by Bad Girl Lovers, Inc. You could get a free three-minute sample, and then the full video was $9.99. Surprisingly, it didn't interest me, and I moved on to our local news. We were down in the office before Louie. Amazingly, the coffee pot was turned off, but then I remembered that I had done that last night before taking Morton on his walk. I made a fresh pot and was sipping coffee and checking out the apartment building across the street with my binoculars. Since no one was on display, that only took a minute or two. No doubt that would be the first of a number of disappointments during the day.

I watched as Louie pulled in behind my car. I placed the binoculars back in my desk drawer and then filled Louie's coffee mug as I heard him groaning up the stairs.

"Coffee's on your desk," I told him as he stepped into the office. He gave me a wave and settled into his desk chair. I grabbed Morton's leash and told Louie we'd be back in an hour. I followed yesterday morning's route, only this time, I drove all the way down to River Boulevard and parked. We took a short walk along the path and settled onto a park bench within sight of my car. I kept an eye on the intersection where I was parked in the hope that Gretchen Donahue and her dog Timmy might show up.

I had just stood after twenty minutes and was about to walk Morton back to the car when they suddenly appeared. "Come on, Morton, Timmy," I said. "Timmy." I don't think he understood me. In fact, I was sure he didn't, but he trotted along at my pace anyway. As Gretchen and Timmy crossed the street and stepped onto the path, I called, "Hi, Gretchen. Wow, two days in a row. How are you two?"

Morton barked, and Timmy responded.

"Oh, my goodness, Dev. How wonderful. I was hoping we might see the two of you. Are you heading back to your car?"

"No, we're in the midst of our walk. Would it be all right if we joined you?"

"We'd love it," she said as Morton and Timmy began playing with one another. We took the same route on the path as the day before.

"How did your day go yesterday?" I asked.

"Oh, you know. You just keep your head down and get the job done."

"Yeah, I suppose. Do you work down by the capitol?"

"No, our department has an office downtown, but it's not in the capitol complex, and it's the odd day that I'm even in the office. Most days, I'm checking things all over town. I'm probably in the courthouse more often than our own office. I'll be in a couple of different banks today and tomorrow going over records."

"Are you an attorney or an accountant for the state?"

"No, nothing like that. Just checking and double-checking things. It's really pretty boring, but unfortunately, a necessary evil. Making sure people are playing by the rules."

"I'm sure that would keep you busy seven days a week," I said.

"It does," she replied and didn't comment any further.

"So, how old is Timmy?" I asked, changing the subject.

"Oh, I've had him for six, no wait, it's already been seven years. Time just seems to fly by."

"Yeah, although there are days when it's not fast enough."

She nodded and said, "How long have you had Morton?"

"Oh, a number of years. He was a little more than a year old when I got him. I was watching him for a friend when she was out of town for a week or two, and we became attached, Morton and me. Then she moved out of state, and one night I came home, and there he was tied to my doorknob with a note from her that said thanks for taking him. I couldn't have been happier, and we've been pals ever since."

"Oh, that's a sad tale, but with a very happy ending. You're lucky to have him. Just like I'm lucky to have Timmy."

We eventually walked to Gretchen's house. Along the way, we set up a walking date for the following morning. I continued up the street, and once I checked to make sure she was in her house, I turned at the next corner. We hurried back to my car at the River Boulevard and drove down to the office.

Toward the end of the afternoon, Luther Harris called. He gave me Davy Ruff's address and told me he was going over to Percy's office to keep an eye on his car from 5:00 until whatever time Percy left.

Morton and I joined Louie over at The Spot for a couple of beers and a bag of pork rinds and then went home.

Eighteen

I placed a frozen pizza in the oven and ate half of it, then drummed my fingers on the kitchen counter before I decided to check out Davy Ruff's address. His home was over on the east side of town, on Lawson Ave. It was a small, narrow, two-story white frame house, maybe a hundred years old. There was nothing attractive about the place. The trim and the small porch at the front door were faded red. Both the siding and the trim had lots of peeling paint. The lawn, what little there was of it, was in need of cutting. There were lots of weeds and what appeared to be a dead maple tree along the side of the house. Ruff's pea-green car with the whiskey plates was parked alongside the house on a dirt path with tire ruts just in front of the dead tree. There was a light on in a room at the back of the house that I guessed was probably the kitchen. I drove around the block and down the alley. There was a small lean-to structure that looked original to the house with paint that was peeling just as bad as the house. As I passed the structure, I caught sight of Ruff's car backing out of the dirt path onto the street.

I drove down the alley and back onto Lawson Ave. I caught Ruff's tail lights just rounding the corner at the far end of the block. I sped up the street and then followed him from a block behind. He drove onto Phalen Boulevard, then turned onto Cayuga Street, and, from there, took the entrance onto 35E going through downtown and then west. I was afraid I knew exactly where he was going. Sure enough, he remained on 35E until he crossed the Mississippi and took the Mendota exit. I decreased my speed, allowing two cars to pass me. He followed the road into the lovely little development where Tracey lived. I slowed at the corner and watched as he drove along the street, pulled into her driveway, and parked. He climbed out of his car carrying a brown paper bag that appeared to hold a bottle. He hurried to her front door and rang the doorbell. A moment later, the door opened. Tracey wrapped her arms around him and gave him a long kiss. As she pulled away, he handed her the bag with the bottle and stepped inside. Tracey rubbed his rear with her free hand as he stepped past her and then closed the door.

I checked my dash. It was 9:40. I drove home, decided against having a beer, and turned on the news, just in case I wasn't already in a foul mood. I was in bed before 11:00 and slept fitfully. I woke forty-five minutes before my alarm was set to go off and hit the shower. I debated driving over to Tracey's house to see if Davy Ruff was still there. But then what? There was nothing to be gained other than putting myself in an even fouler mood. And by the way, what was that about? It wasn't like I had a relationship with her. Well, other than business, and that was tenuous at best. I guess I just felt guys like Davy Ruff shouldn't be allowed to be with a woman, let alone a gorgeous woman like Tracey, even if she was a porn star.

We were down at the office a little after 8:00. I made coffee, and then we drove over to Gretchen's house. I parked in front of her place at 8:45. As I stepped out of the car and opened the rear door for Morton, Gretchen stepped out of the house with Timmy. She looked especially fetching, dressed in very nice straight-leg black slacks and a pale pink blouse with the sleeves rolled up on her forearms.

"Well, good morning, and right on time. Wonderful to see you," Gretchen said.

"Good to be seen rather than viewed," I replied.

She gave me a look and then laughed. "Oh, it took me a minute. I'll have to remember that one. You set to do the boulevard?"

"We're looking forward to it," I said, and we began our walk. We chatted about the dogs for a bit, and then I asked, "You mentioned you were at the bank yesterday. Are you thinking of selling or refinancing?"

"What? Oh, no, nothing like that. I'm at banks a couple of times a week. It's part of my job."

"Well, hopefully, it went well."

"Mmm-mmm, I'll know later today. We're looking into an individual, and, well, there seem to be a lot of questions. The more we learn, the more questions arise."

"Sounds tough. I'm just happy if I can balance my checkbook."

She laughed at that. We walked down to the scenic overlook again and then turned around and headed back to her house. "I don't know what your schedule is like, but I baked some blueberry muffins last night. If you have time, we could have a muffin and a coffee on my patio. No pressure if you don't have the time and have to get to your office."

"On the contrary, I'd love it. How very nice of you."

When we arrived at her house, she led us to a side gate and into the backyard. She unclipped the leash on Timmy, and he ran about ten feet in front of us, then turned and barked at Morton to follow. I unclipped Morton's leash, and the two of them ran further into the backyard, dodging and chasing each other across a brick patio and out into the yard. A round table with four chairs was in the middle of the patio. A boxwood hedge lined the back of the patio. A variety of flowers and plants grew along the fence. Off to the left were four wood-framed raised beds. One held tomatoes, another had a couple different types of lettuce, one had squash, and the fourth one looked like it had garlic.

"Do you grow garlic?" I asked.

She grinned and said, "I do. Three different kinds. Come on inside. You can help carry the coffee out. Morton won't jump the six-foot fence, will he?"

"No, and besides, he's having too much fun chasing Timmy," I observed as they chased each other back and forth around the apple tree at the end of the yard.

We went up three steps into the kitchen through the back door. The cabinets were red birch with quartz countertops. A center island held the kitchen sink, and just beyond that was a stove with five burners and a pair of side-by-side ovens below it.

A china plate with four blueberry muffins was on the center island, and two travel mugs stood in front of the coffee pot. "How do you take your coffee?" she asked.

"Just black, please."

She filled both travel mugs with coffee, placed the lids on the mugs, and said, "If you would grab those mugs, I'll carry the muffins, and we can sit out in the sunshine before it gets too hot."

I grabbed the mugs and headed for the back door. Gretchen took something from a cookie jar and then picked up the platter with the muffins. I held the door open by standing against it, and she made her way down the steps. She set the muffins in the center of the table as I placed the coffee mugs in front of two of the chairs.

Timmy and Morton caught sight of the muffins and hurried over.

"Oh, wouldn't you know," Gretchen said, then held out two dog biscuits. Both of them sat immediately, appearing as if they were at attention. She tossed a biscuit in front of each of them. They quickly snapped them up and headed to a distant corner.

"This is so nice of you to do, and you have a lovely garden," I said, looking around.

"My spare time," she said and laughed. "Help yourself to a muffin." She pushed the plate in my direction.

I grabbed a muffin and set it in front of me. Once she took one and began to peel off the paper muffin cup, I did the same, then took a bite. It was delicious, moist, and full of blueberries.

"Oh, these are so good," I said and took another bite.

"Thank you, it's a recipe I got from my mother. I love them, but I have to be careful. I'm more than capable of eating five or six every day. Help yourself to another."

"Oh, I really shouldn't."

"Yes, you should. Because if you have a second one, then I can have another one as well."

"Oh, yeah, well, anything to help out," I chuckled and grabbed my second muffin from the plate.

We had a wonderful conversation about things in general and the dogs. I was tempted to tell her about Ernest Stanton, but I didn't want to ruin our budding friendship. After thirty minutes or so, she said, "Well, I've really enjoyed this. Thank you so much for joining us on our walk and for taking the time to sit and chat. Unfortunately, I have to head out to work."

"Oh, thank you so much, Gretchen. The muffins, the coffee, our chat, the walk. Thank you for going to all the trouble of putting this together. Really, I so appreciate this. It's been absolutely wonderful, and now I should get to the office, too."

"Thank you, Dev. Would you like to take some muffins with you?"

"If I did, I'd devour them before I got to the office."

She smiled at that and said, "Okay, then they're here for another day."

"Morton," I called. "Morton, come on."

Both Morton and Timmy walked over. I grabbed the leash and clipped it onto Morton's collar. "Thank you again, Gretchen. Would it be too much to ask if you're going to do a walk tomorrow?"

She grinned and said, "I was afraid maybe we'd chased you away. Yes, I would love it."

"Same time, and I'll bring the after-walk treat if that works for you," I said.

"I'd love it," she replied and held out her hand.

I took hold of her hand and then leaned forward and gave her a peck on the cheek. She grinned. "Can I help carry things into the kitchen?"

"Not a bother. Go on, get to your office."

I took hold of Morton's leash. She walked us to the gate and then watched as we went to the car. Once I got Morton in the car, she waved and closed the gate.

Nineteen

As we stepped into the office Louie asked, "So everything okay?"

"Yeah, had a nice walk along the River Boulevard. It's a gorgeous day, and I'm actually in a good mood."

"Oh my. You're in a good mood! That is unique."

"Very funny, not. Are you in court today?"

Louie nodded, "Yeah, first thing this afternoon. I'll head down there just before noon and meet up with my client."

"Well, unless something comes up, I should be on my computer for the better part of the day." I settled in at my desk, turned on my computer, and then placed a call to Luther Harris. He answered after a couple of rings.

"Hi, Dev, everything okay?" was how he answered.

"Yeah, no problem. Just a minor update for you." I went on to tell him about following Davy Ruff out to Tracey's last night and described her welcoming kiss and rubbing his rear.

"What? She's giving that idiot action?"

"That seems to be the case."

"How late did he stay?"

"I didn't wait around to see. I was tempted to drive back over there this morning, but I didn't want to be in a bad mood for the rest of the day."

"You know, since he's a photographer, and he's done work for her, do you think her special service might be the way she's paying the guy?"

"Actually, I never thought of that. I suppose it's possible, but I can't believe she'd have trouble paying whatever he charges. That unit she lives in has to go for eight or nine hundred grand, don't you think? Based on her business, it would seem her basic physical needs are being met."

Luther laughed at that last comment.

"I do know she just released another video in the last day or so. She seems to be making money. I guess I don't get it, but then that shouldn't be a surprise."

"Well, interesting. I think I'll keep this information tucked away for the time being. I can't see any benefit in mentioning it to Percy."

"Have you ever been past Ruff's house?"

"No, I know he lives somewhere over on the east side, but I've never gone past the place."

"It's a frame structure, maybe a hundred years old, and I'd say the worst house on the block. A weed garden for a lawn, a dirt area he parks in with a dead tree. The place hasn't been painted in at least twenty years, and all the paint is peeling off the house. I'm glad he's not my neighbor."

"Your description isn't surprising. Who knows what she sees in the guy other than his camera."

"Okay, just wanted to bring you up to date."

"Thanks, much appreciated, Dev. Enjoy your day."

"You do the same, Luther," I said, and we disconnected.

Louie headed down to the courthouse, and Morton and I walked up to Roosters. I got a BBQ pork sandwich for me and a beef shoulder bone for Morton. Toward the middle of the afternoon, my phone rang.

"Haskell Investigations," was how I answered.

"Please hold while I transfer you to Mr. Ernest Stanton," a female voice said.

The phone clicked a couple of times, and then a grouchy voice said, "Stanton."

There was a long pause while I waited for him to say something else, finally, I said, "Hello, Mr. Stanton?"

"Haskell, is that you?"

"Yes, sir."

"Oh, I'd like to see you tomorrow morning at 9:00. I want you to fill me in on what you've learned regarding Gretchen Donahue."

What I'd learned is she appeared to be a very nice person, Morton liked her dog, she was private about her work, and I was out of patience with Stanton. "Actually, I'm still checking into Miss Donahue, sir. I wonder if we could move this back to the following week, and I—"

"The following week? No, I don't want to wait that long, and you've had more than enough time to investigate. I insist that people in my employ preform. Now I want—"

"She's a very private person, sir, and given her employment with the State Attorney General's Office and the Financial Crimes Task Force, it's not as if information is easily available."

"In other words, you haven't done anything."

"On the contrary, sir, I've looked into a number of areas, but given what I've just mentioned, the information is not exactly forthcoming."

"Find a way to make it forthcoming. I'll expect to see you at 9:00 tomorrow."

"I already have a meeting scheduled for tomorrow morning, and I—"

"9:00 tomorrow morning, and I want information," Stanton shouted and hung up.

I looked at my desk phone for a moment and then hung up. I suddenly felt as if a weight had been lifted from my shoulders. I could call Stanton and tell him I quit, but the more I thought about it, the more I would actually enjoy telling him in person. I wouldn't be able to meet him at 9:00. Morton and I were scheduled for a walk with Gretchen and Timmy. Oh, and by the way, I was bringing the treats for after our walk.

Louie arrived back in the office forty-five minutes later. Once he'd recovered from his stair climb, he said, "You're looking happy."

"Thank you. I feel wonderful. I received a phone call from your friend, Ernest Stanton, this afternoon."

"Okay, first of all, he's not my friend."

"Oh, yeah, sorry about that. Believe me. He's not my friend either."

"What happened? Did he threaten you?" Louie asked.

"Not in so many words. He's just someone I don't enjoy working for, and so, one of the benefits of being self-employed is I'm not going to work for him anymore."

"You told him you quit?"

"No, I'm saving that for my in-person visit tomorrow morning. I just feel very relaxed after deciding it's not worth the hassle."

"It wouldn't be the first time I've heard something like that regarding Stanton. He's very impressed with himself."

"That's clearly an understatement. It should be interesting," I said.

"Well, please keep me posted."

I took Morton for a walk before we met Louie in The Spot. He was gracious enough to buy a congratulatory round to celebrate my decision to cease investigating for Ernest Stanton. He apologized three or four times for passing my name on to the guy and then bought another round. Morton and I were home before 8:00 and in bed by 11:00.

Twenty

As usual, I was up before my alarm. I was showered and shaved by the time Morton arrived downstairs. We made a fresh pot of coffee at the office, and then we drove to Kowalski's grocery store and bought four caramel rolls and two large dog biscuits. The rolls were still warm from the oven, and the caramel was still sticky. When we pulled up in front of Gretchen's home, she and Timmy were already in the front yard trimming geraniums in the window boxes.

She was dressed a little more casually than usual today. Wearing nicely pressed white jeans and a light blue denim shirt. As I climbed out of the car, she turned, waved, and set the clippers she was using on a chair on the front porch. She grabbed Timmy's leash and strolled across the lawn to greet us. "Oh, great to see both of you. It looks like we have a wonderful day for a walk."

"Yes, we do, and if you have time, I've got some pastries in the car for after our walk."

"I was counting on it," she smiled.

I took Morton out of the backseat, and we gave the two of them a couple of minutes to go through their meeting and greeting routine. I clicked the fob to lock the car, and we headed for the River Boulevard. Today, we walked past the scenic overlook and continued on for another quarter-mile before we turned around and headed back to the house.

Once in the backyard, the dogs chased around the apple tree, and we stepped into the kitchen. Gretchen filled the travel mugs with coffee while I warmed the caramel rolls for thirty seconds in the microwave. She grabbed the silverware and the mugs, and I carried the plates with caramel rolls and a paper bag out to her patio. As Morton and Timmy approached, I opened the paper bag and tossed a large dog biscuit to each of them. Gretchen and I sat and gossiped, trading stories for the better part of an hour. I offered to warm a second caramel roll for her, but she shook her head.

"They were delicious, thank you, but one is really my limit."

"Well then, I guess we're both sweet enough," I said. "Are you taking the day off? You look lovely, don't get me wrong, but you seem, I don't know, maybe a little more relaxed."

"Oh, thanks. No, actually, we've been putting the finishing touches on an investiga—umm, I mean a particular project we've been working on. I was in the office until almost 9:00 last night, but we're close to finishing up this project. We passed it on to the higher-ups, and they'll review it over the next few days."

"Sounds like tough work."

"We want to make sure there's no stone unturned if that makes any sense."

"Actually, it does. Well, it's served as my good fortune because you look lovely, and today I got to walk even further with you."

"It was nice. It's not very often when I don't have to look at the clock, so on the occasional day when that's the case, I really enjoy it."

"Believe me. I know exactly what you're talking about. Well, I suppose we should head out and let you enjoy the rest of your day."

"To tell the truth, Dev, you've been the highlight of each and every day we've taken these walks. Today was no exception. It was just better because, well, just because."

"Same here. Let me help with carrying some of this into the kitchen for you."

"No, absolutely not. You've done more than enough."

"All right. Why don't you hold onto those last two caramel rolls, and we can have them another day."

"I will. How about tomorrow?"

"That would be perfect," I said.

Gretchen suddenly stepped forward, took hold of my arms, and kissed me on the lips. Not just a quick peck but more of a lingering kiss. I was thinking of pulling her closer when she pulled back, smiled, and said, "Thank you."

"No, thank you, Gretchen," I replied.

The same as yesterday, she led us to the gate and then watched as we walked to the car. Once I got Morton settled on the backseat, I turned to give her a wave. Today, she blew me a kiss and then waved and smiled.

I waved back and called, "Thank you." I climbed behind the wheel, tooted the horn, and headed down to the office. It was after 11:00 by the time we arrived. I got Morton settled and then left a note for Louie telling him I was heading over to Ernest Stanton's office. After Gretchen's kiss, I felt great.

Once I arrived, I got a not-very-friendly look from the receptionist as I stepped into the Rebel Investments lobby. Her look suggested she was very much aware that I was over two-and-a-half hours late for my appointment. "Hi, my name is Devlin Haskell, and I'm here to see Mr. Stanton," I said and smiled.

"I believe your appointment was scheduled for 9:00, Mr. Haskell. I'm not sure Mr. Stanton has any time at the moment."

"Would you mind checking? It will only take me a minute or two to bring him up to date. I've had a busy morning."

She seemed to think about that and said, "If you'd wait here. I'll see if he has time." As she spoke, she looked me up and down in a dismissive manner. I smiled and bit my tongue. She was back two minutes later. "Mr. Stanton is just finishing up. If you'd have a seat," she nodded toward the couch and chairs. "He'll see you shortly."

I settled into one of the wingback chairs and waited, then waited some more. There wasn't a clock in the lobby, and I didn't want to pull my cell phone out to check the time. Eventually, the receptionist's phone rang. She answered it, said, "Yes sir," and hung up. "If you'd follow me, please. Mr. Stanton will see you now."

I followed her back to Stanton's office, past the offices with people on their phones. She knocked on the door as she opened it then held the door for me as I stepped in.

Stanton was seated at his desk wearing a gray suit, a starched white shirt, and a red tie. A large Starbucks cup, a yellow paper napkin, a three large wrappers for burritos were piled in front of Stanton, and a squirting plastic bottle of barbecue sauce were in front of him on the desk. There was just an inch or two of a burrito left on the wrapper. Which meant I was sitting out in the lobby for the better part of a half-hour while he ate his massive lunch. He picked up the napkin, dabbed at his lips, and said, "Thank you, Ashley. If you'd close the door, please, on your way out."

I watched as she closed the door behind her. I stepped toward Stanton's desk. "No need to sit down, Haskell. At no surprise, you've only served to be a major disappointment. We had a 9:00 meeting, which you failed to show up for. You didn't bother to inform me. You haven't done anything I've asked, and frankly, I'm considering canceling our work agreement."

Apparently, this was the point where I was supposed to beg. Instead, I said, "I think that's probably a very good idea, Ernest. The little I've discovered does not show you in the best of light, and I don't wish to be involved. I'm canceling our verbal agreement. I won't charge you for the effort I've made thus far. I wish you all the very—no, on second thought, forget that last part. Let's just quietly bring things to a close."

Stanton's eyes widened, and he half-shouted, "Who in the hell do you think you are? Do you have any idea who you are dealing with? Do you have any idea in that tiny brain of yours the opportunity you are about to throw away?"

"Please calm down, Ernest. You don't need—"

"Calm down," he shouted, this time full force as his face grew red. "You're telling me to calm down?"

"Please lower your voice, Ernest. I don't—"

"You don't know what you're doing, you miserable, stupid bastard. I'll have you know—"

"Watch yourself, Ernest. It would be best if you calmed down, or you're going to learn manners the hard way."

"Manners? I'll teach you manners," he screamed as he jumped to his feet and pounded a plump fist on the desk. He knocked over the Starbucks cup in the process. His chins jiggled, and his massive belly strained against his shirt, as a wave of creamy coffee spread out across the desk. I expected him to pop a button or two on his shirt at any moment. "You worthless piece of scum. See what you've done." He grabbed the yellow napkin and attempted to soak up the coffee, but it only made the mess worse. "See, see, see what you've done! You're unfit, Haskell. You're an idiotic fool and—" He tossed the coffee-soaked paper napkin in my direction.

It landed at my feet. I picked it up and made a quick, underhand toss back toward him. It splattered against his starched white shirt and his red tie.

"You just assaulted me, Haskell. I'm going to sue your dumb ass for assault."

"Ernest, you are—"

"You cannot do this to me. Do you hear? I won't let you do this," he shouted. His face was now scarlet, his entire body was shaking, and he appeared ready to explode.

"Ernest, you need to—"

"Don't you dare call me by my first name. You are not worthy."

"Okay, Mr. Stanton, you need to calm down. Stop shouting and listen to me. I quit. I'm not working for you. I will not charge you for my time and effort. Goodbye," I said, then turned and stepped toward the door.

"You don't leave until I tell you to go," he shouted.

"Enjoy your day, Ernest," I said as I opened the door and stepped out of the office.

"Get back here, Haskell. I'm not finished with you. Haskell, you can't quit. I fired you. Haskell, do you hear? Haskell? Haskell?" he screamed as I made my way past the open office doors. People behind their desks stared wide-eyed at me as I walked by.

"Thanks, Ashley," I said to the receptionist when I stepped into the lobby.

She just nodded and watched as I walked past her desk and out of the office.

Twenty-one

I stopped at McDonald's on the way back to the office for a little celebration. I ordered three cheeseburgers and a chocolate shake and ate them in my car. Louie returned to the office shortly after I arrived.

"Did you already meet with Ernest Stanton?" he asked as he waved my note.

"Oh, yeah," I said and filled him in on the details, finishing up with, "all that yelling and screaming, the guy better watch it, or he's going to give himself a heart attack. Apparently, he has never, ever been told 'no' before."

"That sounds like the person I know. He's very used to getting his own way. Can you imagine working for someone like that?" Louie said as he shook his head.

"Funny you say that. No one in that office looked very happy. Man, talk about issues. Everyone was staring at me as I walked out. I don't know. Maybe they hear that kind of explosion all the time. It was crazy."

"But you're okay?"

"Me? Oh yeah, I'm fine. I only wish he would have come at me. I would have loved to punch him and then maybe kick him when he was down."

"Yeah, careful, Dev. That's all you'd need is an assault charge. Just be glad you're finished with him. Oh, and my apologies again for passing your name on to him. I knew he was nuts, but I had no idea."

It was almost 5:00 when Louie turned off his computer. "What do you say to a beverage over at The Spot?" Louie asked as he stood from his desk chair and pushed it up against the picnic table.

"I think that's a wonderful idea. Let me just take Morton for a walk, and we'll join you in about fifteen minutes."

"I'll see you over there," Louie said and headed out the door.

I grabbed Morton's leash. At the moment, he was up close and personal with the beef shoulder bone I got at Roosters the other day. He looked over at me holding the leash, then back at the shoulder bone, and finally got up and hurried over.

"Good idea, pal. There will be pork rinds at the end of the walk." That last comment got his tail wagging, and we stepped out of the office. I waved at one of the hairdressers in the Salon across the hall. She gave me the finger and laughed. We went down the stairs and stepped outside. Just as the door closed behind us, a squad car pulled into the bus stop, and the window on the passenger door lowered.

I peeked in, saw my pal Dan Sexton, and said, "Hey, Danny, how are things going? Everything all right?"

"Not really, Dev. I'm supposed to take you downtown."

"Take me downtown? What's going on? I don't get what—"

"They just told me to take you down, man. I think someone filed an assault charge. They're thinking it's a little strange but hoping you'll help sort it out."

"An assault charge? I haven't—Oh my God. Was this filed by a guy named Earnest Stanton?"

"I don't know, Dev. Honest, I think they just want to talk to you. This ain't an arrest if that's what you're thinking, but apparently, there's a team of high-buck lawyers pushing this, and you know how that works."

"Okay, umm, is it all right if I take my dog over to The Spot?" I said and nodded across the street. "My office mate is in there, and he'll watch Morton. They're not going to lock me up, are they?"

"No, they just want to hear your side and get this off the desk as soon as possible."

"Okay, give me a minute or two. Park over there by the side door, and I'll be right out. Are you going to have to cuff me?"

He shook his head. "No, you'll have to ride in the back, but I won't cuff you, well, unless you want me to. I've heard you might like that."

"Oh, please. I'll be out in just a bit," I said. Morton and I hurried across the street. Probably for the first time ever, I moved just as fast as Morton. I kept pace with him along the bar and around the corner to where Louie was seated on his stool.

"Oh, wow, that was fast. Did you guys even go for a walk?"

"No, look, something just came up I gotta deal with. Can you watch Morton? I don't know how long this is gonna take, but hopefully not more than an hour or two."

"Everything all right?"

"Not really. Apparently, pain-in-the-ass Stanton filed an assault charge against me. The cops would like to talk with me, so hopefully, I can get rid of this thing before it gets any worse."

"You want me to head down there? I'll provide you with legal representation and—"

"I don't think that will be necessary. They just want to have a friendly talk."

"Okay, if it even begins to go the other way, you shut the hell up, call me, and I'll be down there in ten minutes."

"Thanks, Louie. Hopefully, it won't come to that, but much appreciated." I handed Morton's leash to Louie. Louie reached over, pulled a bag of pork rinds off the rack, poured some in his hand, and reached down to Morton. "Go on, Dev, get out of here. We'll be fine."

"Thanks, Louie," I said and stepped out the side door. Sexton was parked at the curb. As I stepped out of The Spot, he climbed out from behind the wheel, walked around the squad car, and opened the rear door for me.

"Hop in, Dev. Think of it this way, I'm just your chauffeur," he closed the door once I was inside. I slid across the seat. There was wire mesh between the front and backseat, and no door handles on the inside of the doors.

He climbed behind the wheel just as a couple I knew came around the corner and happened to glance into the squad car. They both stared with surprised looks on their faces as Sexton started the engine and pulled away. I gave a quick wave as we drove down the street, and they hurried into the bar.

It took all of ten minutes before we were pulling into the secured lot alongside the police station. Sexton parked in a numbered spot, climbed out, and opened the rear door for me. "You doing okay?" he asked.

"Yeah, I'm just not too excited about this."

"Can't say as I blame ya. Look, they just want to hear your side. Think of it like this, if nothing happened, you could be able to file against him for false charges."

"Yeah, I suppose. Oh hell, I never should have offered to help this guy. He's been bad from the start."

"Come on, let's get it put to bed," he said and took me in through the secure door. We took the elevator up to the third floor and walked down the hall to the interview rooms. As we approached, I heard a couple of guys laughing. Sexton held the door for me, and I stepped in. There were three guys seated at the metal-topped table. My friend and head of homicide, Lieutenant Aaron LaZelle, was not one of them.

"Well, look who's here. Sorry to interrupt your evening, Dev. I don't know if Sexton told you, but we have something that came across the desk, and we're thinking we want to nip it in the bud. Grab a seat," Detective Sherman said. He was almost my height, with dark hair and a neatly trimmed beard. I hadn't seen him, or for that matter, Detectives Mejia and Russell, the other two guys, since a memorial service last March.

I knew Sherman from a case a couple of years back. Some idiot had been exposing himself along the light-rail lines as the trains went past. I'd helped to catch the guy, which sounds like some major undertaking, but in all honesty, the guy couldn't run too fast with his pants down around his knees, so it was no big deal.

"Take a seat, Haskell," Mejia said and pointed at the only empty chair. It was obvious this wasn't your typical interview following a crime. The door to the room was still open. Sexton had settled into a chair against the far wall and, and at the moment, he was texting someone on his cell phone. There weren't any files on the table, only a laptop computer.

"Are one of you guys going to read me my rights?" I asked as I sat down. I was beginning to relax but still on the cautious side of things.

"It wouldn't do any good," Russell said.

"Here's the deal, Dev," Sherman said as he typed in a password, and the screen on the laptop flashed on. "I got an email from an acquaintance at an investment firm called Rebel Investments. Are you familiar with them?"

"Are you kidding me, Ernest Stanton? President of that place. A royal pain in the ass. What did he do, accuse me of stealing millions from them?"

"Actually, no, he's thinking of accusing you of assault but hasn't officially filed, yet," he said and then turned the laptop toward me. It displayed what looked like a cell phone image of Stanton sitting at his desk. The coffee stain from the napkin I tossed was clearly visible on his white shirt and red tie. Then there were the two streams of blood flowing from his nose and over his lips.

"What the hell? I didn't do that. I would have loved to punch him, but I didn't. Someone else must have hit him in the nose. That looks," I pulled the laptop closer and studied it for a moment, then shook my head. "Guy's, that's not blood. It looks like sauce. I was in his office and had to wait for like a half-hour before he'd see me. He had eaten a burrito for lunch. The wrapper and a final bit were on his desk, along with a coffee that he knocked over and a plastic bottle of barbecue sauce. That's probably what he used. He just squirted the sauce on his upper lip. Is this for real?"

They all laughed. Then Sherman said, "A guy I know sent this to me. Apparently, Stanton has been cautioned not to send this, but someone in that office got ahold of the image and sent it to my pal, and he sent it to me. So you know this Stanton douche?"

I nodded and said, "He hired me to investigate a woman named Gretchen Donahue. She works for the State Attorney General's office, investigating financial fraud. I met her and decided I wasn't going to pursue my investigation of her. I told him I quit, and he didn't have to pay me."

"Did you give him any information regarding Donahue," Mejia asked.

I shook my head. "No, not a word. He was pretty pissed off at me. He shouted at me on the phone yesterday before he hung up on me. Then, like I said, he kept me waiting for a half-hour this morning. He tossed the napkin at me that he used it to soak up the coffee he spilled. I tossed it back at him, and that caused the stain on his shirt and tie. He was screaming and all red-faced, and I was afraid he was going to have a heart attack or a stroke."

"He might be filing a lawsuit for dry-cleaning costs," Russell said, and everyone laughed.

"So, is this thing going to happen. The assault charge?"

Sherman shook his head. "Based on what my friend told me, no. This Stanton guy has been cautioned not to file. Just a warning to you. He's a successful guy, and apparently, money is no object, so be careful. You said you quit?" I nodded. "Well, keep your distance and be careful."

We chatted for another ten minutes. I thanked them for letting me know, and Sexton took me back out to the squad car.

Twenty-two

When we walked out to the parking lot, I stepped over to the rear passenger door. "You're not going to handcuff me, are you, Sexton?" He shook his head and then opened up the front passenger door and chuckled. "You guys went to a lot of trouble to pull this off," I said as I climbed in.

"We'll be telling this story about you for the next twenty years," Sexton said. He drove me back to The Spot and pulled right in front of the entrance. "Just a quick word on this Stanton guy, Dev. This thing was so stupid it never would have worked, and apparently, he either realized it or was told that. But these high and mighty guys, they have a lot of options at their fingertips and a lot of jerks who would like to get on their good side and would gladly go after you. Be careful, dude."

"Yeah, thanks, Danny. I appreciate you guys giving me the warning. I never trusted Stanton, and now I'll be on the lookout."

"If you need any help, you feel something's not right, don't be afraid to get in touch. Okay?"

"Yeah, thanks, man," I said, and we shook hands. I climbed out of the squad car and gave a wave as he pulled away and headed up the street. As I stepped into The Spot, the conversational hum dropped a couple of decibels.

"Dev, everything all right?" Mike asked from behind the bar. "We heard the cops picked you up."

"Yeah, not a problem. They just needed my advice on something."

He looked like he didn't quite believe me but gave me a nod anyway. As I headed over to Louie, I passed two guys who were regulars. "Out on bail already," one of them asked.

"Yeah, they took my credit card, and amazingly it wasn't denied."

"So everything go okay?" Louie asked as I came around the corner of the bar. Morton was lying on the floor. He looked up at me but didn't bother to move. I noticed two empty pork rind bags on the bar.

"Yeah, everything's fine," I said, and then I told him about the image of Ernest Stanton with the barbecue sauce on his face.

"I can't believe he's stupid enough to try something like that. What the—The guy is supposed to be a successful businessman, and he's doing that? Who sent them the image, anyway."

"They didn't give me a name, but it almost has to be someone from the Rebel Investments office. The guy is such a jerk. You can just imagine some staff person getting the image and sending it to a bunch of folks, and then one of them sent it to Detective Sherman. I'm just lucky they picked up on the fact that it was a bogus image."

"Well, that and the fact that they alerted you to it. I'd be careful. It sounds like Stanton realized what a bad idea this was, but that doesn't mean he won't try something else. Don't take it lightly, Dev. Despite this, he's not stupid, and he could do something to make life very miserable for you."

"That's pretty much what the cops told me. God, like life isn't tough enough."

"Here, Dev. On the house," Mike said and placed a beer on the coaster in front of me.

"Oh, thanks, Mike. You didn't have to do that, but very much appreciated."

"I'm just glad everything worked out okay for you. It did, didn't it?"

"Yeah, worked out fine. Thanks for the beer," I said and took a large sip.

He smiled and headed back down the bar.

"Oh man, that was sure nice of him. He didn't do that for me," Louie said.

"I guess you'll have to wait until you get hauled off in the back of a squad car."

We talked for a bit. Louie apologized a half-dozen more times for giving my name to Earnest Stanton and then said, "Let me buy you another beer, Dev."

"Oh, thanks, Louie. But I've got to meet someone tonight, and I should probably head out."

"You're not thinking of paying Earnest Stanton a visit, are you? If you are, I'll buy you beers all night just so you don't do it."

"Thanks for the offer, but not to worry. Stanton is the last person I want to see tonight, or any other night for that matter."

"Okay, keep thinking like that. I'll see the two of you in the morning," Louie said, then waved his empty glass at Mike, who was pouring beers down at the other end of the bar.

I gave a wave to Mike as Morton and I headed out the side door. I debated dropping Morton off at home, then decided I could probably use his support. We drove over to Gretchen's house. Along the way, I practiced what I planned to say to her. By the time I pulled in front of her place, I was no further ahead. Morton was excitedly pacing back and forth in the backseat. I opened the rear door, grabbed his leash, and we walked up to the front stoop and rang the doorbell. I could see the light on in the kitchen through the front door window.

A moment later, Gretchen opened the door. "Oh, Dev? Is everything okay?"

"Hi, Gretchen. Yeah, everything is fine. It's been a bit of a crazy day. Would it be all right if we came in for a few minutes? I mean, if we're not interrupting anything."

"Oh my God, by all means, come in. You'll give me a much-needed break from watching the news. Talk about depressing," she said and opened the door. "Actually, Timmy is out in back. Could I talk you into a glass of wine, and we can sit out there? Have you had dinner? I've got some leftover lasagna I could warm up and—"

"No, thank you. I'm sure it's lovely, but I've had my dinner," I lied. "I will take you up on the glass of wine."

"Well then, come on back to the kitchen," she said and closed the door behind us. As we stepped into the kitchen, Gretchen said, "Let Morton out into the backyard. They can chase one another around while I pour the wine."

As I walked Morton to the back door, his wagging tail slapped against the bottom cabinet doors. I unclipped his leash, opened the kitchen screen door, and Morton jumped off the steps and into the backyard.

Gretchen had two wine glasses on the counter and was in the process of taking a wine bottle out of the refrigerator. "You're sure everything is okay, Dev? You seem, I don't know, preoccupied or a little quiet."

"Yeah, everything is okay. I would just like to tell you about my day or, well, actually about the past few days, and I—"

"Are you in some kind of trouble?" she asked as she stopped filling the wine glasses and stared at me.

"Let's sit down outside," I said.

She set the wine bottle on the counter and said, "You're not going to tell me you're married, are you?"

"Married? Who in their right mind would have me?"

"Outside, Mister," she said, but then she smiled, topped up my glass, and followed up with, "I think you're a pretty nice guy."

We settled into the two chairs at the table facing the backyard. At the moment, Morton and Timmy were chasing each other back and forth around the apple tree.

Gretchen set her wine glass on the table and asked, "So, what exactly is going on?"

"Promise me you'll listen until I've finished telling my story, and then I'll answer any and all questions."

"All right," she said as she crossed her arms, settled back, and stared. Not a good start.

"Okay, so here's what I think is going on. First off, I should tell you I'm a private investigator. That's what I do for a living. I've been doing it for years and—"

"And you're investigating me? Why in the hell didn't you—"

"Gretchen, calm down. No, I'm not investigating you," I said.

Twenty-three

My storyline took an immediate U-turn. "See, I've, umm, been investigating a guy, a tech guy. I've been hired by his soon-to-be former wife. She suspected the guy of having an affair because he was gone seven days a week, from dawn until after 9:00 in the evening. What happened was he started his own company. He now has two employees, and the business is growing. Apparently, he just landed a big contract, so he'll be adding employees and hopefully growing by leaps and bounds. He appears to be a very nice guy, and I can't find anything that suggests he's involved with anyone or anything other than building his business.

"His wife, the woman who hired me, turns out to be a porn star and is in the process of doing the same thing, building her business. She's released five or six thirty-minute videos that I think she sells for $9.99 on a number of different online sites, and she—"

"Her name wouldn't happen to be Tracey Wilde, would it?"

"Well, she, wait, what did you just say?"

"I asked you if her name was Tracey Wilde? Her company goes by the name of Bad Girl Lovers, and her stage name, if you can call it that, bedroom name might be a better term. Her stage name is—"

"It's Racey Tracey? How did you know that?" I asked.

"Oh my God, Dev, how shocking, what a small world! God, I can't believe it."

"But how do you know about her? If you're into porn, that's okay with me. In fact, I've got some DVDs you might like, and I subscribe to a site called Triple X—"

"Stop, please," she said as she held up her hand. "No, for your information, I'm not into porn. Never have been and never will be. God, I just can't believe this. The reason I know her name is, and I should preface by telling you that I work for the State Attorney General's office in the Financial Fraud division. I'm on the Financial Crimes Task Force. The investigation we've been working on for the last two months concerns a man by the name of Ernest Stanton."

"Ernest Stanton? The same Ernest Stanton who is the president of Rebel Investments."

Gretchen sat there with her mouth open and a stunned look on her face. Eventually, she grabbed her nearly full wine glass and gulped it down. She shook her head and asked, "How, in God's name, do you know Ernest Stanton?"

"Oh, that's interesting. Now it's making sense. Apparently, Tracey passed my name onto him," I lied. "Yeah, that's what happened. He wanted me to investigate a couple of people. First of all, I didn't have the time. But second, and more importantly, I didn't like him, so I went to his office late this morning after our walk, and I told him I didn't want to work for him and that I wasn't going to charge him for the work I'd already done."

"And how did that go?"

"I'm guessing by the fact that you even asked that question, you know what his reaction was." I went on to describe Stanton's meltdown and how I thought he was liable to give himself a heart attack or a stroke. Gretchen just kept shaking her head and smiling. She literally laughed out loud when I told her about being driven down to the police station and the image of Stanton with the barbecue sauce that was supposed to be blood.

"Oh. My. God. Oh, Dev, that's hilarious. Our report is that Stanton is hiding funds in the Bad Girl Lovers organization. He bought a car worth six figures and donated it to the president of the organization."

"Would that be a blue coupe that Tracey drives?"

She nodded. "Actually, it's a Mercedes Benz AMG SL 63 Roadster. They go for around two hundred thousand dollars. That doesn't even begin to cover the home she has in Mendota that supposedly serves as the studio. Then there are the various junkets to Europe, the far east, down to Mexico and Hawaii, all in the line of business.

Oh, I'm still laughing about the barbecue sauce disguise. If only he'd actually filed a lawsuit. Okay, I need another wine, and I'm swearing you to secrecy on all of this. You cannot mention this to anyone, and in fact, I'd probably lose my job if they found out I'd talked to you about it."

"I promise I won't say anything to anyone. Can I ask you one thing, actually two things?"

"You can ask, but I can't promise I'll answer."

"Fair enough. First, is Tracey Wilde going to be a part of the lawsuit against Ernest Stanton if it ever happens?"

"It will happen, and I've already said too much."

"Okay, and my second question is, in your investigation, did the name Davy Ruff ever come up? He's a sometime photographer of Tracey's."

"Davy Ruff, that name doesn't ring a bell. Is he a local photographer?"

"Yeah. I don't really know anything about him other than he has photographed Tracey. As far as I know, he isn't the cameraman on the videos, although he could be, and I just don't know."

"I'm going to get the wine bottle, and you're going to empty your glass by the time I get back. God, I can't believe it," she said, shaking her head as she stepped back into the house.

I was just glad everything worked out for me as far as telling her about Stanton. I figured it had to be something like this, but I had no idea an investigation was this far along. No wonder Stanton was virtually apoplectic with rage over my decision to quit. But then, even if I continued an investigation, it certainly wasn't going to change anything. One thing did come to mind. Based on the information Gretchen mentioned about Tracey's company being the collector of Ernest Stanton's investment funds, it might be a good idea to distance myself from Tracey as well.

Gretchen came back out to the table a few minutes later carrying an ice bucket with two bottles of wine, one of which hadn't been opened. She had a plate with crackers and a wedge of what looked like brie cheese.

We laughed, traded stories, and didn't mention Tracey Wilde or Ernest Stanton for the rest of the night. I woke up as she climbed out of bed and headed for the bathroom. Although the drapes were closed in her bedroom, I could see that the sun was up. She stepped back into the room wearing a silk kimono robe that went down to her knees.

"Oh, you're awake," she said, cinching the robe around her waist. "I'm going to put the coffee on and make some toast if you'd like. I've got homemade bread."

"Yes, I'd love it."

"Get dressed and join me downstairs," she said and then left the bedroom.

I spotted my jeans and shirt draped over a chair in front of what looked like a makeup table. I remained in bed for a long moment, attempting to recall the later portion of the evening. At least things had gone well as far as mentioning Ernest Stanton. Now I just had to remember to stick to that version of the story. I slowly climbed out of bed and got back into my clothes. There was no sign of Morton or Timmy, and I wondered if we'd left them outside overnight.

I spotted the two of them once I was down in the kitchen. They were in the backyard, stretched out in the sunshine. "Did Timmy and Morton sleep outside last night?" I asked just as Gretchen handed me a large steaming mug of coffee.

"No, they slept down here in the kitchen last night. Both of them curled up in Timmy's bed," she said and pointed at the large black cushioned bed with the name 'TIMMY" embroidered in white across the front of the pillow. "I put food and water dishes out on the patio, but I'm guessing they'll be in the process of multiple naps after whatever they did late last night."

"Thank you for the incredible story and the lovely evening," I said.

"Oh, and the same to you, very enjoyable," she said, raising her eyebrows. "Just remember. You are sworn to secrecy on a number of different levels."

"I'll remember. I'm going to see if I can acquire that image of Mr. Stanton with the barbecue sauce supposedly dripping out of his nose. If I can get it, I'll send you a copy, provided you never reveal how it came into your possession."

"Scout's honor," she said, holding up her right hand. I ate a piece of toast with blueberry jelly and finished my coffee. We scheduled a walk for Monday morning. I got a very nice kiss and a thank you at the front door as we left. We headed home, and I took a long hot shower and shaved. Since it was Saturday, I closed my eyes for a short nap around 11:30. I woke up an hour and a half later, made lunch, and debated calling Gretchen for dinner. I decided that maybe it wasn't my best idea, and Morton and I took a long walk through the neighborhood. I made a grilled cheese sandwich for dinner and thought about calling Tracey. I immediately decided Monday would be the better day to talk to her and bring my investigation of Percy to a close.

Sunday was more of the same, a leisurely day on my own with Morton. We took a long walk down along the river. I threw a number of sticks, and Morton chased the occasional squirrel. Fortunately, he missed the skunk I saw over near the base of the limestone bluffs. We hiked about a mile and a half up to Hidden Falls and then back to the car. For a dinner treat, I roasted some salmon on the grill, and believe it or not, I read a mystery book until I got to the point where I was drifting off to sleep and went to bed.

Twenty-four

L ike always, I was up before my alarm, showered, shaved, and we were down in the office and got the coffee going by 8:00. We headed over to Gretchen's for our walk and rang her doorbell. Timmy almost immediately appeared on the couch, looking out the window and barking. I rang the doorbell a second time, and Gretchen still didn't appear. I walked around to the side gate and entered the backyard. As we rounded the corner of the house, she stepped out of the garage.

"Oh, Dev and Morton. I'm sorry, I was just loading some things in the car. Didn't mean to keep you waiting. Let me just get Timmy, and we'll meet you out front."

"Everything okay?" I asked.

"Yes, just enjoyed the weekend so much, I was still in weekend mode when I realized it was actually Monday morning. I've got a work meeting at 11:00, so I'll have to shorten our walk. Sorry," she said.

"Not a problem. Do you want to just skip it today and you can carry on? There's nothing worse than having to rush and gather things up for a meeting."

She seemed to think about that for a moment and said, "Would you mind? It's just turned into a crazy day. I've already had two work related calls."

"Not a problem. We'll leave you to it. I tell you what. See how the day goes, and if you have time tonight, the door is open for dinner at our place. The backyard is fenced, so Timmy and Morton can run around. I'll work up some dinner, probably peanut butter and jelly sandwiches, and you can just relax."

She gave me a look when I mentioned the sandwiches and said, "Would you like me to pick something up?"

"Gretchen, I was kidding. Get on with your work. The offer is open for dinner, and if things remain crazy, it's no problem if you have to cancel at the last minute. Okay?"

She nodded and said, "Thanks, that will be nice. Much appreciated. Hopefully, we'll be over tonight."

"I'll text you my address," I said.

"Oh, don't worry. I've already checked you out," she replied with a smile.

We were back in the office fifteen minutes later. Morton was involved with his beef shoulder bone, and I was studying the two women in the third-floor apartment across the street since they had left their shades up. I was enjoying the view when Louie pulled in behind my car and parked. I filled his mug, set it on the picnic table, and returned the binoculars to my desk drawer. "Fresh coffee in your mug," I said as he stepped into the office. He gave me a wave in return.

"How'd your weekend go?" he asked a couple of minutes later.

"Oh, pretty low-key," I said, not wanting to get into anything regarding Tracey Wilde or Ernest Stanton.

"Any phone calls or emails from Stanton?"

I shook my head and said, "No, thankfully. Maybe he's concluded I'm not worth the effort."

"Let's hope it stays that way."

I went online and sent Jim Sherman an email on his personal site, asking him if he would send me the image of Ernest Stanton. I doubted he would, but it was at least worth a try. I placed a call to Tracey Wilde and ended up leaving a message.

"Hi Tracey, Dev Haskell calling. Just wanted to touch base with you. Let me know a time when we can meet up."

"You going to cut her loose?" Louie asked.

"It's more like I've checked out her soon-to-be for-mer husband, and the guy is working seven days a week. He's not having an affair with another woman, at least from what I've found out. If he was, it would almost have to be a blow-up doll he kept under the bed. The guy is literally working all day, every day, week after week. Everything Luther Harris has told me verifies what I've found out." I didn't bring up Ernest Stanton investing in

Bad Girl Lovers, buying the two hundred thousand dollar Mercedes, or paying for the prime piece of real estate that was Tracey's so-called studio.

I got a text message back from Jim Sherman just before the noon hour. 'Sorry, no can do.' I wasn't surprised, and in fact, it was probably a good thing, otherwise, I'd send or show it to someone, Stanton would find out, and I would end up being sued.

Louie left for a court appearance, and I took Morton on a walk. I still hadn't heard back from Tracey, so after checking the news online, we headed to the grocery store to pick up something for dinner.

The day had a pleasant blue sky. The temperature was in the upper seventies with no wind, and I decided that rather than cook, I would get a quart of a cold bow tie pasta with garlic chicken. I picked up a French cheese spread and crackers for an hors d'oeuvre along with some cookies that looked like they were home baked. I stopped at Solo Vino and got three bottles of wine just in case I could entice Gretchen into spending the night.

I ran the dishwasher, changed the bed linens, cleaned the shower, and put out fresh towels. I went out into the backyard and spent a half-hour cleaning up Morton's debris left over from the last week or two.

It was almost 6:30 when Gretchen phoned. "Hi, Gretchen," was how I answered.

"Oh, hi, Dev. Sorry I'm calling so late. Does the term 'day from hell' mean anything to you?"

"It does, but only because I have about seven of those every week. Oddly, today was not one of them. Can I talk you into coming over to relax and be waited on?"

"Oh, Dev. I would love it. Are you sure it's not too late?"

"Morton just told me you're supposed to bring Timmy."

"Thank you. This is very kind of you."

"Relax and take your time. Get here when you get here. No pressure."

"Sounds perfect. We'll see you shortly," she said and disconnected. She wasn't kidding. The doorbell rang about twenty minutes later. I opened the door, and Gretchen handed me a bottle of wine. Morton barked, and Timmy ran past Morton and headed toward the back of the house.

"Oh God, what a day," Gretchen said.

"Well, come on in, and let's get you started on relaxing. Dinner will be served when you want it. Whether that's now or hours from now, no rush."

Morton and Timmy charged back into the entry, circled us, and headed back into the kitchen.

"Timmy, stop. Timmy," Gretchen shouted.

"Don't worry about it. I'll put them out into the backyard, and they can chase one another to their hearts' content. Come on back to the kitchen."

As we stepped into the kitchen, the dogs were dodging one another. "Morton, Timmy," I half-shouted as I set the wine bottle on the counter. "Biscuit." That word seemed to get their attention, and they immediately came to a stop and quickly settled into the sitting position. I opened the cookie jar where I keep the dog biscuits and pulled out two biscuits. I held them in a way that gave me their undivided attention.

"Hold on for just a moment, Gretchen." I opened the back door and stepped outside. Morton and Timmy were right behind me. I handed them each a biscuit, which they snatched up and quickly moved to opposite corners of the backyard so they wouldn't have to share.

"Can I pour you a glass of wine?" I asked as I stepped back into the kitchen.

"Tonight, I'd be happy to drink it right out of the bottle," she replied.

"I just opened a bottle and it's in the refrigerator. I'll put the bottle you brought in there and let it chill, and we'll start on the cold one." I'd already set the wine glasses on the table along with the platter of crackers and cheese. "Grab a seat," I said, and she did.

I poured two glasses of wine and set one in front of Gretchen. I set the other glass on the table and then stepped behind Gretchen in the chair. "Sip your wine and begin to relax. I'm just going to give you a little shoulder and neck rub and—"

"Oh, don't worry. You don't have to do…. oh my, that does feel good. Really good."

"I can feel it in your shoulders, Gretchen. You're tensed up. Your muscles are tight. You just relax, sip some wine, and think happy thoughts. You know, like Monday is behind you, and Timmy and Morton are chasing one another, so they'll be exhausted in no time. We're not on any schedule, and I have a wonderful meal waiting whenever you decide you want it." I massaged her shoulders back and forth, rubbed her neck, and then returned to her shoulders.

"Oh, God, you are really good. Where did you learn how to do this?"

"I actually took a class a number of years ago. Isn't it amazing how just a little bit can really help to minimize, if not completely erase, the tension? Especially in the work environment where we're all on our best behavior when what you'd really like to do is kick some idiot a half-dozen times or climb in a boat and row across a lake and back."

"Amen to that first thought," she said and took another sip of wine.

"Take some slow deep breaths and just clear your system. It really helps." She took a deep breath, exhaled, and took another deep breath. She did it a couple more times, and I could actually feel her shoulders and neck begin to relax. She had a few more swallows of wine, and when she emptied her glass, I massaged her shoulder for another minute, then grabbed the wine from the refrigerator and refilled her glass.

"Oh, that was wonderful. Thank you so much."

"My pleasure. I've found over the years that it can really make a difference in just helping to calm down after a stressful period. Shall we step outside and check on our better halves?"

Twenty-five

Morton and Timmy were lying in the grass, both of them working on chew toys. "Oh, Morton, nice job of sharing," I said.

"You have a lovely place," Gretchen said, looking around. "How old is your house?"

"It was built back in 1885. I bought it quite a few years ago. The neighborhood has been on the rebound, with younger families moving in and redoing the houses. It's been a lot of work. Slowly but surely, the neighborhood has improved. The city, in its wisdom, seems to still have the thought, "Who would want to live in an older house?"

"Well, I think it's a lovely area. Your place is really nice."

"After dinner, I'll give you the five-minute tour. Why don't you take a seat at the table, and I'll bring our cheese and crackers out."

"Oh, I can help."

"I know you can, Gretchen. But take advantage of the moment and just relax. I'll be right back."

I set my wine on the glass-top table and hurried into the house. I was back outside with the French cheese spread and crackers thirty seconds later. Gretchen had already spread some cheese on a cracker and popped it into her mouth by the time I sat down. That suggested to me that she was, indeed, beginning to relax from whatever she'd had to deal with today. I reminded myself not to ask what had been going on.

We chatted about general things. She asked a number of questions about the neighborhood and the houses around my place. We ate half the cheese, and then I brought out the bow-tie pasta with the garlic chicken in a large serving bowl.

"Oh my God, Dev. Don't tell me you made this."

"All right, I won't."

"What? You did?" She took a forkful once I dished up a plate. "Mmm-mmm, delicious. Did you make this?"

Seeing no advantage in telling the truth, I said, "Actually, I make it all the time. I simply cook the chicken in a little garlic and use some olive oil and garlic on the pasta."

She seemed to believe me, took another forkful, and said, "This chicken is delicious."

"Garlic chicken, what's not to like?" I replied.

We ate and talked. Each had a second helping, and I made sure her glass was never empty as we worked our way through the second bottle of wine. I topped up her glass again, cleared the plates, and brought out the cookies.

"Oh my, don't tell me you bake, too."

"One of the many things I love to do," I lied.

There were eight large chocolate chip cookies on the plate. I had two. Gretchen ate four, but in such a polite way that I never thought she had eaten that many until I looked at the plate and there were only two left. We went into the kitchen once the mosquitos came out. I opened the third bottle of wine, gave her another shoulder rub, and we eventually headed up to bed. I turned off the alarm and woke at my usual time the following morning. Gretchen was still asleep.

I picked up my clothes, closed the bedroom door behind me, and stepped over Timmy and around Morton, stretched out in the hallway. I showered and shaved and was downstairs on my second coffee when both dogs appeared in the kitchen. I gave them each a head scratch and let them into the backyard. A moment later, I heard the shower turn on upstairs. I set the kitchen table and arranged the makings for French toast. Gretchen was downstairs a half-hour later. Her hair was combed, and she wore a small amount of makeup. I had a glass of water, a bottle of aspirin, and a mug of coffee waiting for her on the kitchen table.

"Oh, thank you for the aspirin. How much wine did we go through last night?"

"Let's just leave it at enough. Can I talk you into some French toast for breakfast? The maple syrup will get some sugar into your system and help eliminate any headache you may be dealing with."

"You've talked me into it. Our best friends are outside?"

"Yeah, they came down a little while ago. Food and water are out next to the back steps. Last I saw, they were stretched out and enjoying the sunshine."

I made four pieces of French toast, placing two pieces on each plate. I put the plates on the table and topped up our coffees. Gretchen poured a heavy dose of maple syrup onto her plate and dug into her French toast. Her phone rang a few minutes later. I glanced at the clock on the stove. It was 7:10. She pulled the phone out of her purse, checked the screen, and apparently sent the call to voicemail.

"It's okay if you want to step in another room or even outside and take a call," I said.

"No, I'll call back after breakfast. Oh, my thanks to the cook. I didn't realize how hungry I was," she said and shoveled more French toast into her mouth and smiled.

"I can make some more. It will just take a minute."

She shook her head. "Oh, thank you, but we should be on our way. I've got to get Timmy home and head to work." She stabbed the last two bits of French toast, ran them through the puddle of syrup on her plate, and smiled. "This has been so nice, Dev. Thank you for everything, the massage, the garlic chicken pasta, last night, and now this. I'm in full recovery after yesterday, although it might be a day or two before I have another glass of wine. Let me grab Timmy, and we'll get out of your hair."

"Don't feel you have to rush out on my account."

"No, it's going to be another crazy day, and I need to get moving. Thank you," she said as she stood, leaned over, and gave me a kiss. She grabbed her purse and Timmy's leash and gave me another kiss.

"Thanks for coming over," I said as we stepped into the backyard. Morton and Timmy were still lying in the morning sun. They both raised their heads and trotted over. She clipped the leash onto Timmy and gave Morton a scratch behind his ear. I got a kiss on the cheek, and Morton and I followed them to Gretchen's car in the driveway.

It was my turn to blow her a kiss and wave as she backed out onto the street. As she pulled away, her phone was up against her ear.

I loaded the dishwasher, washed the frying pan, and went upstairs. I put on a different shirt, and we headed down to the office. It was just a little after 8:00, and I made a fresh pot of coffee and was scanning the apartment building across the street when Louie pulled in behind my car. I turned on my computer so it would look like I had been working, filled his coffee mug, and settled in at my desk.

Once Louie had rested up from his climb to the second floor, he asked, "How did your evening go?"

"Oh, fine. I worked late, checking out some things for Tracey," I said. "In fact, I'm going to call her in just a bit and see if she'll have time to meet with me later today. God love him, but her soon-to-be former husband is in his office all day, every day. I'm not coming up with anything different, and I'm going to suggest we bring my investigation, such as it is, to a close."

"So the good news is he's not involved in an affair," Louie said.

"Yeah, that's good news regarding Percy, the husband. It's bad news for Tracey, who I suspect was looking for some sort of financial remuneration. Given her line of work, the video company, she'll be lucky if she doesn't end up paying him."

"Is he looking to request that as part of their divorce?"

"Not that I know of, but I have absolutely no knowledge of what he's looking for. I think there's a pretty good chance he'd like to just part ways, wish one another luck, and get on with their lives."

Louie shook his head, packed up his computer bag, and five minutes later was on his way down to the courthouse. I thought for a minute and placed a call to Tracey. I ended up leaving a message. I called again an hour later. I hung up rather than leave another message and decided to drive over to her home.

Twenty-Six

After taking the exit off the 35E bridge. I was waiting for the light to change so I could turn onto Highway 13 and head toward the development where Tracey's home was located. At the opposite end of the Highway 13 bridge that went over 35E, a pea-green Chevy-Spark made a left turn onto the entrance ramp for 35E and headed back across the river. The odds that the driver wasn't Davy Ruff had to be close to zero. I was tempted to follow him, but then what?

The light changed. I drove across the bridge and continued on into the development where Tracey lived. I pulled into her driveway, climbed out, and rang her doorbell. The door opened a moment later.

"I knew it, Davy. You couldn't stand to wait, and you're back for more—Oh, Dev, what are you doing here? We didn't have an appointment, did we?" She was dressed in a red, loosely tied, half-sleeve silk robe. She pulled the belt tighter and stared at me with wide eyes.

"Hi, Tracey. No, we didn't have an appointment. I'm sorry. I hope I'm not interrupting anything. I called a few times, left a couple of messages, and thought, since

I didn't hear back, I'd just stop by and hope I caught you with a free moment or two. If you want me to stop back later, I can do that."

"Oh, no, no, umm, come on in. Can I get you a coffee? I've got some on."

"Yeah, I'll take a cup. How are things going?" I asked as we walked through the living room, past the fireplace with the painting in the gold gilt frame of naked Tracey and the tattoo. We walked past the couch where she had passed out while she'd been on the phone. I followed her into the kitchen. Two plates with remnants of scrambled eggs and sausage were on the kitchen counter. A number of wine bottles, a Maker's Mark bourbon bottle, a half-dozen empty glasses, and three take-out pizza boxes from Bogey's bar covered the center island. The sink was filled with more plates and glasses. Apparently, there'd been a party last night, or maybe it had been the night before, and Tracey just hadn't gotten around to cleaning up.

She reached into the sink and grabbed a coffee mug. She turned on the faucet and rinsed out the mug twice. She filled it partway with coffee, then grabbed the bourbon bottle. "Can I top it up for you?"

"Oh, thanks, but I've got a lot to do, so I'd better not." I saw no point in mentioning it wasn't quite 10:00 in the morning.

"Well, suit yourself," she said and handed the coffee mug to me. Red lipstick was still on one side of the mug, so I switched hands, turning the mug around. "I think

I'm going to need something a little stronger." She filled her coffee mug at least a third of the way with bourbon and topped it up with coffee. She leaned back against the counter, looked at me for a moment, raised her eyebrows, and said, "So, what were you hoping for?"

"Actually, Tracey, I wanted to stop by and bring you up to date on my investigation of Percy."

"Oh, God, Percy. Talk about Mister Boring. Okay, what have you found out?"

"Well, pretty much what you just said. He works seven days a week, from early in the morning until late at night. I've followed him home, and other than the occasional stop at the grocery store, he goes straight home. He arrives home around 9:00 or 9:30. He's at work the following morning around 6:00 AM. He has two employees, a man and a woman. He works all day on his computer. He apparently has one or two clients and is hoping to get more, but all he does is work. I haven't found the slightest hint of a relationship with anyone."

She took a big swallow from her mug. "So what you're telling me is he's working his ass off and not making any money."

"I honestly don't know how much money he's making. I can tell you he appears to be working very hard. Like I said, seven days a week."

She shook her head, seemed to think for a moment, and finally said, "Damn it. I was hoping when he wanted to just split everything fifty-fifty that he was hiding something from me. Now you're telling me he's not making any money, and he's working seven days a week?"

"What I said was I don't really know what his financial status is. I can tell you he's driving a Chevy Equinox that's five years old. He's living in an apartment in the attic of a house on Lincoln Avenue, and his office consists of one medium size room in an old converted four-story factory building without any windows. I would guess less than half of the spaces are rented in the building. It's not what you'd call a high-class location."

She took another sip. "You know, you're making it sound like he might be coming after me for money."

"No. If I implied that, I didn't mean to. I'm just telling you what I learned. In fact, what I plan to do is send you my bill. There's no point in you having to pay me for any further investigation when I'd just be coming up with the same information. He doesn't appear to be in a relationship with anyone. He works seven long days a week, every week, and he currently has just one or two clients."

She seemed to think for a moment, then nodded and drained her mug. She poured more bourbon into the mug, topped it off with coffee, and said, "How would you like to be paid?"

"You don't have to pay me now. I'll send you a bill for whatever your down payment doesn't cover, and you can just cut me a check once you get the bill."

She grinned and began to loosen her silk robe. "There might be other ways to pay. Possibly services rendered? A unique lifetime experience, pure pleasure, your choice."

"No, a check or cash will be fine," I said and set my lipstick-stained coffee mug on the counter. "Well, thanks for the coffee. I'll get that bill sent out in tonight's mail. I guess it's good news that he doesn't appear to have cheated on you, and he just wants the best for both of you."

"That sounds boring," she said and slurped more coffee from her mug.

"That's life, I guess. Hey, I'll let myself out. You have a good rest of the day."

"I plan to enjoy myself, Dev," she said, accentuating the word enjoy.

"Thanks, Tracey," I said and hurried back into the living room and out the door. I locked the driver's door as soon as I closed it. I quickly backed out of her driveway and headed back into the city. I decided to drive past Davy Ruff's house. Fifteen minutes later, I turned onto Lawson Street. There was the city's ugliest car parked in front of the dead maple tree on the dirt path with the tire ruts. I drove past and figured Ruff was probably lying in bed with an ice pack on his lap.

Louie was back in the office when I stepped in. He looked up for a half-second and asked, "How's your day going?"

"I just put the Tracey Wilde account to bed, pardon the pun."

"You told her you were finished?"

"I told her what I learned about Percy Riggs, basically that he works seven days a week, long hours every day, and that it's my impression I won't be learning anything else. I told her I'd send her an invoice."

"She's okay with that?"

"More or less. She would have liked to hear he was making millions and she could receive a monthly or annual payment. The fact is, right now, she might end up paying him."

"Did you tell her that?"

"I might have hinted at it. I'm just ready to get some distance from her. She's beginning to strike me as a bit of a loose cannon. Plus, she seems to be paying her photographer with services rendered, and he seems to be considering her as his one and only. Just looking down the line, I have the feeling there's bound to be trouble, and I don't want any part of it."

"Sounds like you might have dodged the proverbial bullet."

"I hope so." I sat down at my desk and called Luther Harris. He answered on the second ring.

"Hi, Dev. What's up."

"Just calling to see if you might have time for lunch today. I've brought my dealings with Ernest Stanton and Tracey Wilde to a close, and I want to give you an update."

"Everything go okay?"

"More or less."

"Yeah, let's meet for lunch, and it's my turn to buy. You know where the Gopher Bar and Grill is?"

"Yes, I do. It's been a while since I've been there."

"Well, nothing's changed. I'm just on my way to check in with Percy. How 'bout we meet at the Gopher around   12:30?"

"I'll see you there. Feel free to pass on the fact that I'm done with Tracey and Stanton."

"Thank you. I'll do that," he said and disconnected.

Twenty-seven

Morton and I went for a walk just before noon and then drove down to the Gopher Bar. The place is famous, or maybe infamous, as a dive bar, for its crass treatment of customers and the wonderful Coney Island hotdogs. Any deviation from the menu or special request would be met with an expletive or two. I'd known George Kappas, the owner. He was a no-nonsense guy, a good businessman, and on top of all that, a very nice person. Unfortunately, he'd passed away six months ago.

I was about ten minutes early, and luckily, I was able to grab a table from two guys who were just leaving. I ordered a beer and waited for Luther Harris to arrive. He stepped in the door promptly at 12:45, by which time I was on my second beer.

"Hi, Dev, sorry I'm late. Percy had all sorts of questions, most of which I didn't have answers to. You been here long?"

I shook my head and said, "I just got here myself."

"Okay, my day is looking better already." He turned toward the bartender two tables away and behind the bar, pointed at my beer, and signaled one.

"What kind of questions did Percy have?"

"He wondered what I'd found out about that Davy Ruff character."

"Is he an issue for Percy?" I asked.

Luther shook his head and said, "To be honest, I haven't had the time to check him out. We're both keeping an eye on him. I've spotted his car a couple of times. Once in the morning, just driving past Percy's office, and twice in the evening as Percy drove home, both times at night. I think he became aware of my presence and pulled away."

"Is Percy doing anything that would get Tracey upset?"

"Not really. If you mean has he filed for financial support or accused her of being unfaithful, he's done nothing along those lines. There's a part of me that thinks she may be upset because he went along with her decision to split, and she expected him, or maybe even hoped that he would put up a fight. I don't know, but maybe she thought he would do anything to make her stay."

"Well, I can add something to that equation." I went on to tell him about my going over to Tracey's earlier in the morning. About seeing Davy Ruff's car heading back into town and Tracey answering the door, thinking I was Ruff for a half-second. "The kitchen looked like there had been a party the night before, and she was drinking coffee mixed with bourbon before 10:00 in the morning. I don't know if that's a daily undertaking or if it was just a one-time event. Maybe the previous night's get-to-gether was to celebrate something, a business success, or the fact that she wasn't pregnant. Who knows?"

"So she and Ruff are in a relationship now?"

A waitress stepped over and set a mug of beer in front of Luther. "You two ready to order?"

I looked over at Luther. He nodded and said, "Give me two Coneys with everything."

"Same for me," I said, and she headed back to the bar.

"You were asking about a relationship. I think it de-pends on which one you talk to. Ruff probably believes they're in a relationship. I suspect Tracey is paying him via physical interaction rather than cash. I would guess he attended whatever get-together was at her place last night, and he apparently spent the night. Which is why she answered the door saying, 'You're back for more' and then realized it was me. I'll say it again, my concern is that Ruff may view Percy as competition, for lack of a better term, and I think he's capable of doing almost an-ything that would eliminate competition."

"Is Ruff the reason you quit working for Tracey?"

"Not really. I quit because I'm convinced Percy is working all day, every day, seven days a week. He's not involved with anyone unless it's business. That said, beautiful woman that she is, I just, I don't know, there's something there that I can't quite put my finger on. But it concerns me, and I don't want to be part of some disaster down the road."

"Well, she is a porn star."

"That doesn't bother me. In fact, in a way, I find it one of her stronger points."

The server appeared with our Conies and set the plates down in front of us. "You guys need anything else?"

"I'm good," Luther said.

"Me, too."

She set the bill down next to Luther, who immediately grabbed it and said, "I got this, Dev."

"I'll get it, Luther. I think it's my turn to buy."

"You know, I think you're right," he said and handed me the bill. I could have kicked myself for making the stupid comment. "As long as you brought up Davy Ruff, I told Percy we were getting together for lunch, and he asked me to pass on an offer."

"What kind of offer?"

"I'm basically keeping an eye on Percy. You have turned out to be an upstanding individual. The fact that you are no longer working for Tracey will make you appear even better as far as Percy is concerned. He would like to hire you for the purpose of checking into or, maybe I should say, keeping an eye on Davy Ruff. If you're interested, he would like to have you drop by his office later today." Luther looked at his watch. "It's just a little after 1:30. He'll be in his office for another eight or nine hours."

"Really? He wants to hire me?"

"Yeah, if you can fit him in."

I chuckled about that. "After cutting the cord with Ernest Stanton on Friday and Tracey this morning, my desk is pretty clear. Do you know what time he grabs lunch?"

Luther shook his head. "He really doesn't. He packs a lunch and eats a sandwich and maybe an apple or something while he's working."

"Should I call him and set up a time?"

Luther seemed to think about that and shook his head. "No, I don't think that would be necessary. He's working nonstop and dealing with things that pop up all the time. Just knock on the door and step in and be prepared to talk to him while he's typing code or something on his computer. You'll like him. He's a nice guy."

"Yeah, he seemed nice during the sixty seconds I was in his office."

That got a laugh from Luther. "Don't forget he was basically playing you. He knew who you were. But you must have made a good impression because now he'd like to hire you."

"Thanks, Luther. I'll head over there as soon as we're finished."

"Thank you for doing that. Running around searching for Davy Ruff has been a real pain in the rear for me. Oh, and welcome aboard."

We finished up. I paid the bill and tacked on a five-dollar tip. We chatted outside on the sidewalk for a minute. I told Luther I would keep him posted, and we headed for our cars.

Twenty-eight

fter driving over to Percy's office I parked a couple of rows away from his car. I made a quick glance around the parking lot but didn't see any sign of Ruff's pea-green Chevy Spark with the whiskey plates.

I took the elevator up to the fourth floor and walked down the hall to number 412. As I opened the door, Percy looked up from his computer screen and smiled.

"Well, Mr. Haskell. I just got off the line with Luther a few minutes ago. He told me you were going to stop over."

"As you probably know, we met up for lunch, and he mentioned you might need some help," I said and gave a quick glance at Percy's two employees.

"I should introduce you. These are my local employees, Laquesha Adams and Jonathan Green. Team, this is Private Investigator Dev Haskell. He'll be taking over Luther's effort, keeping an eye on Davy Ruff. Please, Dev, have a seat," he said and nodded at the worn leather chair beside his desk.

Laquesha and Jonathan gave me friendly nods as I stepped over tangles of electric cords on my way to Percy's desk.

"Thanks, nice to meet you," I said and settled into the chair next to the desk.

Percy extended his hand, and we shook. "So Luther told me you had an update on Mr. Ruff."

"Yes," I said and told him about seeing Ruff's car and Tracey answering the door, thinking I was Ruff coming back for more.

He shook his head and said, "She's definitely changed. That said, I guess so have I. Interesting. So, aside from the event this morning, what do you know about Ruff?"

"Not an awful lot. I've been past his house. I know he has whiskey plates on his car, which, fortunately, is a vehicle identifiable from a mile away. I know that he does photography work for Tracey, and I may be mistaken, but after the episode this morning, she apparently pays at least part, if not all, of his fee via very personal, physical interaction."

Percy nodded but didn't seem to have a reaction beyond that. "And you are no longer employed by Tracey?"

"That's right. I brought that to a close this morning. It was the reason I stopped at her place. She had hired me to check you out, and I basically told her that you are a workaholic, working twelve to fourteen hours a day, seven days a week."

"That would not have been anything she didn't already know."

"Yeah, that was pretty much the reaction I received. Tell me what you know about Davy Ruff."

"Here's what I've been able to obtain online," he said as he turned in his chair and then handed me two pages stapled together. "Glance through it. You probably already know most, if not all, of this information."

It was basic information beginning with Ruff's address. He purchased the home in 2015 for $89,000 dollars. Ruff was a 2010 graduate of Carleton College in Northfield, Minnesota. He graduated with a bachelor's degree in photography. He had been employed by two advertising firms, the St. Paul Pioneer Press newspaper, a fashion magazine, and the Minneapolis Art Institute. That added up to five different companies over eight years before he began his own company, Fantasy Foxxx, in 2019. He was in a car accident in 2020 and was charged with a DWI in 2022, which accounted for his whiskey plates. He was charged with assaulting a woman in 2021, but the charges were later dropped following an out-of-court settlement.

"Interesting information. May I hang on to this?" I asked.

"It's yours to keep, Mr. Haskell."

"Please, call me Dev," I said.

"Only if you call me Percy."

"It's a deal. So, what am I getting into on this? Do you simply want me to, shall I say, monitor Davy Ruff and make sure he stays out of your hair?"

Percy smiled and nodded. "That's correct. If he has a relationship with Tracey, that's really none of my business. I simply want him kept away from our facility, from me, as well as Laquesha and Jonathan. Unless you see him doing something seriously illegal, don't get involved. If he's driving intoxicated, assaulting someone, or robbing a bank, yeah, by all means, call the police. Otherwise, keep your distance."

"I don't need to know your hourly involvement. I just want to make sure he's out of our hair for the foreseeable future. We're in the process of bringing aboard a large client. I want, no, I mean we need to be able to focus, and I do not want to spend our time either dealing with Mr. Ruff or worrying about what he's up to. You have my permission, not that you need it, to share any and all information with Luther Harris as well as the authorities. Any questions?"

"Not at this point. It's possible I may have some in the future."

"Feel free to call or come here in person, whatever works best for you. In addition, you do not need to contact me daily. As long as you keep an eye on him and he's not interfering with our business, I'll be happy. You may send me or deliver an invoice to me at the end of every week. As you already know, I'm here seven days a week."

I nodded, said thanks, and headed out of the office. As I opened the door, I called, "Nice to meet the two of you," to Laquesha and Jonathan.

I got smiles and a wave in return. On the way to my car, I searched the lot for the pea-green Chevy Spark. Thankfully, I didn't see it. I climbed behind the wheel, pulled out my cell phone, and called Luther Harris.

"How'd it go, Dev?" he answered.

"Very well. I just wanted to thank you for setting things up with Percy."

"Oh, believe me, I didn't set anything up. I'm sure he has a file full of information on you. He brought you on board because he liked what he learned about you. He's wonderful to work for. He lets you do things your way as long as you accomplish whatever he asks of you."

"Well, thank you very much. I'll be looking into the daily activities of Davy Ruff and keeping an eye on him."

"Congratulations. Anything I can do to help, just let me know."

"Same from me. If I can help, just give a yell, Luther."

I hopped onto Highway 280, headed north to 36, and then took Snelling Avenue to County Road B2 and the Best Buy store. The store had a half-dozen different trackers for sale. I got a Space Hawk GPS tracker for eighty-nine dollars because it had a surface magnet and no SIM card, so if Ruff ever discovered the tracker, it couldn't be linked back to me. I took the long route back to the office and drove past Ruff's house once more. His car was exactly where it was the last time I drove past, and I figured he was probably fast asleep following his activity with Tracey the previous night. Still, I played it safe and drove past rather than risk being spotted attaching a tracker to his car in the middle of the day.

Back at the office, I went online and set up a monthly subscription on the tracker. For the princely sum of twenty-five dollars a month, I would be able to track Ruff's car on my cell phone. I was trying to think of an easier way to make money than sitting at my desk, watching the women in the apartment across the street, and tracking Ruff on my cell phone. I couldn't come up with a better way. Now, all I had to do was attach the thing to the ugliest car in town.

I took Morton for a walk toward the end of the day, and then we drove past Ruff's house one more time. His car hadn't moved. I drove back to the office, parked in front of Louie's car, possibly the second-ugliest car in town, and we headed into The Spot.

I had a couple beers with Louie, Morton inhaled a bag of pork rinds, and we went home. I placed a call to Gretchen and left a message. "Hi Gretchen, this is Dev. Hope your day went well. Just wondering if you and Timmy would be available for a walk tomorrow morning. No pressure if you can't make it. Thanks."

We watched the evening news and went upstairs. Morton settled onto his bed. I pulled on a pair of black jeans, and even though it was 82 degrees outside, I slipped on a long sleeve black sweatshirt and headed out to the car.

I drove over to the east side and parked a block away from Ruff's house. I walked past his house. His car looked like it hadn't moved all day. The first-floor lights were off, and an upstairs room was illuminated with a flickering blueish light I took to be from a TV. I continued up the block, rounded the corner, and headed down the alley. There was a light on a phone pole illuminating the alley three houses before Ruff's place. It was just after 11:00, and fortunately, no one else was in the alley. I hurried down to Ruff's lot, and just as I stepped into his backyard, a car pulled into the alley.

I hurried in front of the lean-to structure and crouched down as the car drove past. I waited a minute and then hurried over to Ruff's car. I had already turned the tracker on, and I reached underneath the car just below the driver's door and attached the tracker to the car frame. It made a slight bang as the magnet slapped onto the frame, but nothing loud enough to attract any attention. I hurried back into the alley and walked over to the next block and my car.

Once in the car, I turned on my cell phone and brought up the tracking site. Google Maps appeared, and a red dot indicated where the car was parked alongside Ruff's house.

I woke up around 3:30 in the morning and brought up the tracking site. Ruff's car was still next to the house.

I turned off the phone and was back asleep in about sixty seconds.

Twenty-nine

We were down in the office before Louie, as usual. Not for the first time, I turned on my cell phone. Ruff's car hadn't moved from his house since I had attached the tracker last night. I had a fresh pot of coffee on and was watching the two women in the apartment across the street. One appeared to be wearing a silky white t-shirt, and the other was in a bra and a black thong. They were drinking coffee while applying makeup at the kitchen counter and laughing.

The woman with the silky t-shirt brought out a small brush and a container and then made a move that suggested she might pull her t-shirt off. Unfortunately, Louie's faded Ford Fiesta chose that moment to pull in behind my car. "Come on, come on, pull the t-shirt off," I urged in an effort to encourage her, but it didn't seem to help. As Louie headed across the street, I put my binoculars back in the desk drawer, filled his coffee mug, and placed it on the picnic table.

He stepped into the office a minute later and gave me a nod.

"Fresh coffee waiting for you on the table."

He flashed me the okay sign and settled into his desk chair. After a number of slurps, he asked, "Anything happening with Stanton or the woman?"

"You mean Tracey? No, nothing, and fortunately, I haven't heard a word from Stanton. Which reminds me, I need to send an invoice to Tracey," I turned on my computer. I looked at the calendar on my desk, counted the days, did the math, and came up with a figure I thought looked acceptable, then began listing a daily routine. I placed myself at Percy's office around 5:30 every morning, checking again at noon, in the middle of the afternoon, and then from 6:00 until 9:30 or 10:00 every night. It was all pretty much fiction, but I figured with new videos coming out at $9.99 and Ernest Stanton giving her a car worth two hundred grand, Tracey could deal with it.

I typed up a pleasant note, thanked her for the down payment, and printed off the invoice and an envelope. I placed a stamp on the envelope, grabbed the leash, and took Morton on a walk to the mailbox. Along the way, my phone signaled what I thought was a message coming through, but when I clicked on the phone, it turned out to be an alert that Ruff's car was finally moving. The movement appeared to be in real-time, with the image adjusting every three or four seconds. I watched as the red dot headed up Lawson Avenue and took a right at the corner.

Depending on where he was headed, I might have to hop in the car. But the mere fact that I could watch his movements on my phone was great. I wasn't using gas, wasn't racing through town only to find out he was going to the grocery or the liquor store. I tossed my invoice to Tracey into the mailbox, and rather than take the long route, we headed back to the office just in case Ruff headed for Percy's office.

Louie was gone when we reached the office, and I clicked my phone on. Ruff was just moving onto 35E and heading south. I checked again a few minutes later. He was winding around downtown and continuing south. The good news was he obviously wasn't heading toward Percy's office. But, the odds of him making his way to Tracey's house were increasing. Forty-eight hours ago, that probably would have upset me. Now, I just thought it was stupid. Stupid on Tracey's part for dealing with him in the first place. Stupid on Ruff's part because, at the end of the day, he was being used.

I checked four minutes later. He was still heading south on 35E, approaching the bridge crossing the Mississippi. Once on the bridge, the Chevy Spark moved into the right-hand lane and took the Mendota exit at the end of the bridge. I turned off the phone, checked the time on my computer, and made a mental note to check the tracker in fifteen minutes.

My phone rang, Luther Harris. "Hi Luther, how's your day going?"

"Nothing happening, which is just fine. Percy was in the office at 6:15, and all is well."

I went on to tell him about the tracker on Ruff's car and the fact that he was headed toward Tracey's.

"Nice that you can follow him from your office. I wonder if they're filming another video."

"Could be. I don't know for certain, but my sense is Ruff is inserting himself into Tracey's life more than she would like."

"Maybe, but didn't you tell me she had set up a special payment plan for him?"

"Yeah, true. You just have to wonder how much she owes him." We chatted for the next fifteen or twenty minutes. When Luther finally hung up, I checked on Ruff's car. He was parked in Tracey's development but not near her place. His car was parked on the next street over, which I thought was a little strange. I watched the screen for a couple of minutes. Ruff's car never moved, so apparently, he had parked there. That didn't seem to be right. I thought about what to do for a minute, then grabbed my car keys and headed out the door.

Ten minutes later, I'd driven across the bridge and had just entered Tracey's development. I pulled to the curb and turned on my phone. According to Google Maps, Ruff's car was still in the same place. I drove down the street, took a left, and went past a half-dozen lovely brick and stucco homes along a curved street. Suddenly, there it was, the pea-green Chevy Spark looking even uglier than usual, parked between two charming brick homes, each with neatly trimmed lawns and flower gardens. I slowed as I drove past the car. Ruff didn't appear to be anywhere nearby. I thought he might be visiting someone in one of the homes, but if that was the case, wouldn't you park in front of the house or even in the driveway?

I ignored the impulse to let the air out of one of his tires and drove past Tracey's house. It wasn't that far if you cut across the backyards of a number of the houses in between, although I doubted the neighbors in this up-scale development would do something like that. Driving on the curved street and past the lots that were each an acre or two, it took a couple of minutes. As I turned the corner onto Tracey's street, I could see flames in the fire pit on her back patio. That struck me as strange because it was a hot and humid day, and unless she was roasting marshmallows, a fire would be the last thing you'd want.

A large, bronze SUV with tinted windows sat in the driveway. I slowed as I drove past. The words RANGE ROVER were in capital letters across the rear of the vehicle. I recited the license plate number until I pulled around the curve and out of sight of Tracey's house. I grabbed a pen from the console, wrote the license number on my hand, and headed back to the office.

Louie was still out and Morton was asleep on his pillow. I settled in at my desk and placed a call to Dave McGovern at the DMV. "McGovern," he answered in his usual manner.

"Hi, Dave, Dev Haskell. I'm hoping you can check a license plate out for—"

"Dev, do you ever take a break? Maybe I should just call you at the end of every day and get the list of plates you want to be identified."

"Oh, gee, and here I was thinking I would buy you lunch or dinner. How stupid of me."

"Okay, give me her plate number."

"Actually, I don't know who the car belongs to, but it's an awfully nice-looking SUV," I said and read the number I'd written on the palm of my hand.

"Oh, man," McGovern said a moment later. "You have any idea what kind of car that is?"

"Well, it said Range Rover across the back, let me make a guess and say it's a Range Rover."

"Yeah, it's a Range Rover, all right. It's an SV Carmel edition. They go for a couple hundred grand. This one is the property of a company called Rebel Investments."

"Ernest Stanton," I said.

"Yeah, that's the individual listed. How did you know that?"

"Oh, just a guess. I interviewed the guy once a year or two ago," I lied.

"It would be cool to take a ride in that thing, very special."

"Yeah, actually, a friend saw it somewhere and left a note on the windshield offering to buy the thing."

"Well, if he has to ask what the price would be, he can't afford it. They go for up to three hundred grand."

I chuckled and said, "I'm sure my personal check would be acceptable."

"Oh yeah, both of ours," McGovern said. "Hey, I got a call coming in. Let me know if your pal buys it," he said and hung up.

Thirty

So, Ernest Stanton was at Tracey's, and Davy Ruff was parked around the bend. Something was up, and I wasn't sure I wanted to be involved. Instead, I placed a call to Gretchen and ended up leaving another message. "Hi Gretchen, Dev Haskell calling. Just touching base and want to make sure you're doing okay. Give me a call when you have time. I'd be happy to provide another dinner and a shoulder rub for you. Oh, and Morton sends his best regards to Timmy. Take care."

It had been a couple of days since I'd heard from her, and I hoped everything was okay. Given that she was investigating financial fraud, I figured she always had more on her plate than she wanted.

I checked Davy Ruff's car a half-dozen times over the course of the afternoon, but it was still in the same place. Louie wandered into the office around 4:00. We chatted for a bit, and then he headed over to The Spot. Morton and I joined him after we took our walk. Morton had inhaled the first batch of pork rinds, and Mike had just delivered my beer when my phone rang. Gretchen was returning my call.

"I gotta take this," I said to Louie and stepped out the side door since I wouldn't be able to hear over the jukebox. "Hi, Gretchen," I said as the door closed behind me. "We haven't spoken for a couple of days, and I just wanted to see if everything was okay."

"Thanks for your call, Dev. Or should I say your calls? We've been working nonstop on a case. I can't tell you much more than that. It looks like it's going to be a few more days. I'm sorry. We'd love to see the two of you." She sounded as if she was about to cry.

"You just hang in there, Gretchen, and do your best. We're here when you get the time."

"Oh, thank you. Look, I'd better run. We're getting another update. Thank you. Goodbye," she said and disconnected. I thought for a moment and headed back inside.

"Everything okay?" Louie asked.

"Yeah, just someone I was hoping to meet up with later, but it turns out they're busy. So, you never mentioned how your appearance went this afternoon."

Louie filled me in for ten minutes on his court appearance, but I wasn't really paying attention. I wondered if Gretchen's work had anything to do with Ernest Stanton. I finished my beer, and Morton and I headed home. I took some leftover pasta from the refrigerator and ate it from the plastic container. I went onto my cell phone's Google Maps. Davy Ruff was now parked in Tracey's driveway. It was after 8:00, and I wondered if he would be spending the night. Morton and I headed up to bed after the news. I woke up twice in the middle of the night and checked Ruff's car. It was still at Tracey's.

We were down in the office before Louie and made a fresh pot of coffee. Just after 9:00, I checked on Ruff's car. He was driving on 35E, in the process of winding around downtown and heading north. Thankfully, he drove past the logical exit that would have put him onto I-94, heading west toward Percy's office. I checked him a few more times. He was definitely heading home. The next time I checked, the car was parked next to his house. Hopefully, he would be there for the remainder of the day.

Luther Harris phoned just before the noon hour. "Hi, Dev. Thought I'd touch base and check in. Your boy Ruff up to anything?"

"No, he spent the night at Tracey's again. He must have served her with one hell of a bill."

Luther laughed. "God, I can't imagine. There's actually a part of me that feels kind of sorry for her."

"Yeah, I feel the same way. But, that said, I certainly don't want to get involved. Whatever the two of them are up to, keep me out of it. As long as he's spending time with Tracey, he's not trying to cause problems for Percy. How are things with him, by the way?"

"Percy? Well, whoever this new big client is that's coming on board, two people from that company are in town today and tomorrow, laying the groundwork with

Percy and his staff. A couple of his out-of-town employees are here for the meeting, so it's a big deal for all involved."

"Well, I wish him all the luck in the world. I'm keeping an eye on Ruff. He arrived home from Tracey's not too long ago, and hopefully, he'll stay there for the rest of the day. If anything changes, I'll let you know."

"Thanks, Dev. You take care," Luther said and disconnected.

I was thinking about getting something for lunch when my phone rang. I glanced at the screen. Aaron LaZelle, my pal who headed up the homicide division. "Hi Aaron, if you're calling me for a dinner invitation, I'm in, and I think it's your turn to buy."

"Oh, I only wish. Say, if you've got some time, I wonder if you might stop down in the next hour or so? We've got some questions, and we're hoping you can help us out."

He spoke in a friendly tone, but I'd been here before. What he was really telling me was, 'Come down here of your own accord, or I'll have you brought in by two reliable officers.' Whatever was going on, it wasn't along the lines of Ernest Stanton's photo with the barbecue sauce supposedly running from his nose.

"I can be down there in about fifteen minutes. Should I ask for you at the desk?"

"Might be better if you ask for Manning. I'll let him know."

"I'm heading out the door now," I said, and we disconnected. I sat and stared at my phone for a long moment. I didn't know what Aaron's call was about, but it couldn't be good. Asking for Detective Sergeant Norris Manning suggested whatever was going on, Aaron had removed himself because of our relationship as close friends. At least Manning, who used to despise me, had been pretty decent the past couple of years after I helped his son out of a jam. He still played by the book, but he no longer threw the book at me.

I wrote a quick note to Louie, telling him I was down at the station and would be back as soon as I could. I tossed Morton a biscuit and hurried down the stairs. As I went out to my car, I noticed a squad car parked a half-block up the street. I thought for a half-second about waving and quickly decided that would be pushing my luck. The squad car followed me at a distance until it was fairly obvious I was heading to the station. When I next checked the rearview mirror, it was just turning off onto Kellogg Boulevard.

I pulled into the parking lot across the street from the station and entered the building. I asked for Detective Manning at the front desk.

The sergeant at the desk, Tim Reynolds, knew me and said, "Manning? You sure you want to see him?"

"Yeah, he's expecting me."

Reynolds shook his head and, just under his breath, said, "Don't say I didn't warn you."

A few minutes later, an officer opened the security door and called, "Haskell? Devlin Haskell?"

"Yeah, right here," I said as I hurried over to him. A number of people in the waiting room watched me as I rushed past. A couple of people shook their heads. I was sure they'd been there for a number of hours, maybe even longer, waiting to see someone, provide information, or report something, and here my name was called after three or four minutes. At the moment, I would have gladly traded places with them.

I'd seen the officer holding the door open, but I don't think we were ever introduced. "Hi, thanks, Dev Haskell," I said and held out my hand.

He responded with a nod but didn't bother to shake my hand or introduce himself. He looked around and asked, "Are you here on your own?" Which immediately sent a red flag up.

"Yeah, it's just me. I'm probably the most boring guy you'll deal with this week."

He gave a shrug as if to say, 'Okay, if that's the way you want it,' suggesting I should have a lawyer with me to keep me from screwing up.

I followed him along the hall to the elevators. We rode up to the third floor and walked down the hall that led to the interview rooms. The same hall my cop pal Dan Sexton had led me down, telling me they just wanted to hear my side of Ernest Stanton's picture. Not for the first time, I wondered if Stanton had pulled something that they were taking a lot more seriously this time around.

A uniformed officer was standing outside the door of Interview Room Two. This time, the door was closed, and I didn't pick up on any laughter coming from the room. The uniformed officer opened the door, and my escort, who didn't shake my hand or introduce himself, said, "Grab a seat at the table, and Detective Manning will join you in a moment." I stepped into the room and had only taken a couple of steps toward the metal-topped table when I heard the door close behind me.

Thirty-one

After sitting down on the far side of the table. The first thing I thought was that there could be someone, or a number of people, on the other side of the tinted glass watching me. The second thing that came to mind was that I still had my cell phone, and I wasn't handcuffed, so apparently, I wasn't under arrest. At least not yet. I thought back and was pretty sure Tracey hadn't filed a charge against me. Stanton might have been pissed off at me for not discovering some crime Gretchen Donahue had committed, but since I wasn't going to send him a bill, I didn't think he had filed a complaint of any sort, which left Davy Ruff.

I thought about Luther Harris's image on his website. Him supposedly in his office at the fancy desk with all the law books, the stack of files, and the desktop computer. Since Davy Ruff was a photographer, could he have faked images of me stealing something, selling drugs, or maybe with an underage girl?

The door suddenly opened, and Detective Manning stepped in, followed by a guy I didn't recognize.

"Mr. Haskell, thank you for coming down on such short notice," Manning said and shook my hand.

"Good to see you again, sir," I said and followed up with, "How is your son doing?"

Manning smiled. "He's working for Medtronic and liking it. More importantly, they seem to like him. Thanks for asking."

As he settled into a chair across the table from me, he said, "This is Justin Dorc. He's with the state. We're looking into a situation and hope you might be able to help us out."

Dorc extended his hand and said, "Nice to meet you, Mr. Hassle, err, Haskell."

He sounded like meeting me was the farthest thing from nice. I shook his hand anyway and said, "Pleased to meet you. What can I do to help?"

"We're aware you have been hired by a firm known as Rebel Investments, and I believe you report to a gentleman by the name of Ernest Stanton."

So there it was. Stanton had probably fingered me for stealing funds or insider trading or a dozen other things. Thinking he wouldn't do anything, wouldn't come after me, had been just too good to be true. No surprise. I made note of the fact that Manning didn't read me my rights, and all the equipment on the four-wheel rack against the far wall was turned off. No lights were showing, which meant nothing was being recorded.

"I was hired by Mr. Stanton, but in short order, I found that I did not enjoy working for him. Although he suggested I would be able to pursue my own line of investigation, he wanted to involve himself. I had spent some time looking into things and told him that I had discovered nothing along the lines of his initial inquiry. I told him that I would not be sending him a bill and left his office."

"Based on the reports we received from a number of Stanton Investment employees, they described your meeting as extremely contentious."

"Yes, I would say that's correct, all on the part of Mr. Stanton. I did not raise my voice, swear, or at any time threaten Mr. Stanton. He was shouting at me to the point I was afraid he was going to have a heart attack or a stroke. He was red-faced and appeared to literally be shaking. He was furious at me for attempting to explain that, based on my experience, there was no merit in his investigation. He continued to scream even though I asked him to stop. Finally, I opened the door and walked out of his office. He continued screaming at me as I made my way into the lobby and left the office."

"What was the line of your investigation?"

"He somehow had received information that the State Attorney General's office was investigating him for financial fraud. I don't know how he came upon that information. As far as I know, they may have informed him of their investigation and maybe requested a meeting or something. I know they were investigating. I do not know if they have since charged Stanton with anything."

Manning glanced over at Dorc.

"How, exactly, did you go about investigating the State Attorney General's office?" Dorc asked.

"I didn't. I did look online for any indication that there were questions regarding Stanton or his firm. I didn't find anything. I have a friend, a Private Investigator, who has a client involved with computer tech. I asked him to have them see if they could find anything, but they were in the process of bringing a new client, a large new client, on board and didn't have the time nor inclination to look. Based on all that and, frankly, Stanton's attitude, I decided after forty-eight hours that I didn't want to work for him, and as I told you, I quit."

"What were you charging Stanton?" Dorc asked.

I shook my head. "We never discussed my fee, and in the end, I told him I would not charge him for the time I spent."

"Do you know any individuals employed at Rebel Investments?"

"No. I was in the office twice for a total of maybe ten minutes. The only other person I spoke with was the receptionist. Her name is Ashley. I don't know her last name. We probably spoke a total of a dozen words to one another over the course of my two visits to the office."

"Do you have any investments, Mr. Haskell?"

"I don't make the kind of money that would allow for investments," I replied.

Manning waited for a good ten seconds before he asked, "Do you have any more questions, Mr. Dorc?"

Dorc seemed to think for a moment and then shook his head. "No, I guess not. If something comes up, would you mind if we contacted you again, Mr. Haskell?"

"Not at all, happy to help. It's just that I don't know anything beyond what I told you. If you wish to contact me, the department here has my name and number."

"Do you have a business card?"

"Not with me. If you want to give me your card, I'd be glad to send you my contact information."

"If you would, please," Dorc said as he reached inside his suit coat and pulled out a state business card.

"Let me get someone to escort you back down to the Lobby," Manning said. He walked over to the door, opened it, and spoke to the uniformed officer. "Haskell, he'll take you back to the lobby." I nodded at Dorc and headed for the door. As I passed Manning, he gave me a pat on the shoulder and said, "Thank you, sorry to take up your time."

"Nice to see you again. Give my best to your son," I said and followed the officer to the elevator. We didn't say anything on the way down to the ground floor. "Thanks," I said as he opened the door to the lobby for me, but I never got a reply. I climbed into my car and drove back to the office. I parked behind Louie's car, glanced up and down the street, but didn't see a squad car.

Instead of going up to the office, I walked over to The Spot. Two senior citizens were having a beer at the bar. Mike didn't clock in until 5:00. Jimmy was behind the bar this afternoon, and I said, "Hi, Jimmy, you mind if I use your phone for a second? My cell isn't working."

"Not a bother. Help yourself, Dev. You want a beer?"

"Oh, I'd love one, but I'd better take a pass. Thanks all the same."

I pulled my cell phone out, brought up Gretchen's cell phone number, and punched it into The Spot's phone. After three rings, I got dumped into voicemail. "Hi, Gretchen, Dev here. Would you call me please, at your convenience? I had something happen this afternoon that you should probably know about. Maybe don't mention this call to any of your workmates. Thanks," I said and hung up.

Jimmy gave me a funny look as I put the cell phone back in my pocket.

"I can make calls on my cell, but I can't hear what people are saying," I said.

He chuckled and said, "Good luck with that."

I went up to the office. Louie was working his way through a stack of files. He looked up as I stepped in. "Everything okay, Dev? That note you left seemed to suggest something wasn't right."

I went on to tell him about my meeting with Manning and Dorc from the state.

"Sounds a little crazy. You think they were looking into your meeting up with Gretchen and the fact that you were working for Stanton at the time?"

"That was one of my initial thoughts, but they never mentioned her name. Never asked me anything like, did I know anyone in the Attorney General's office? They seemed totally focused on Ernest Stanton, but other than working for him for a couple of days, obviously, I don't know much. I told them I didn't like working for him, that I quit, and I wasn't going to send him a bill. That was pretty much it. Manning was there with the guy, and I could tell he was getting rather fed up with the guy's interview not really going anywhere. The whole thing couldn't have lasted more than fifteen or twenty minutes. They didn't read me my rights. They didn't record any-thing. On my way out the door, Manning thanked me in a way that sounded more like an apology."

"You going to tell Gretchen about this?"

"I just put a call into her from The Spot. I didn't want my phone number showing up on her call report. I left her a voice message."

"Might be best to talk to her in person, just in case they record her phone conversations. Given the depart-ment she's in, that's not too far-fetched."

"Good advice, Louie, thanks."

Thirty-two

Toward the end of the afternoon, even though my phone would sound the alarm if Davy Ruff moved his car, I kept checking on it. Each time I checked, it was still parked next to his house. I was thinking about taking Morton for a walk and heading over to The Spot when my phone rang. I didn't recognize the number but answered anyway. "Haskell Investigations."

"Oh, aren't you sounding professional," Gretchen said.

"Oh, Gretchen, sorry, but I didn't recognize the number."

"That's because I'm calling from a nurse's station at United Hospital."

"United Hospital? Is everything all right?"

"Oh, yeah, not to worry. I'm actually going over some records, but I got your message and thought it might be a good idea to call from this number rather than on my cellphone. You said you had something happen. Are you okay?"

"Yes, and that was probably an improper use of the English language on my part. I was asked to come down to the police station earlier today. It turned out to be a somewhat informal interview in that it wasn't recorded, and they didn't read me my rights or anything like that, but I was questioned by a guy named Justin Dorc. He works for the Attorney General's office, and I wondered if you knew him?"

"Justin Dorc?"

"Yeah, do you know him?"

"Yes, unfortunately. What in God's name did he want? He's, he's, well, let me just say, he's in his own little world."

"Funny you should say that. He was asking somewhat vague questions, and as I left, the detective who was in the room with us told me he was sorry for taking up my time."

"No surprise. Dorc is aptly named and absolutely inept, yet somehow, he has managed to remain employed in the department for years. He must know someone higher up, or maybe more than one bigwig."

"I was wondering if it would be possible to meet up and give you a full report."

"Yes, absolutely. When were you thinking?"

"If tonight would work for you, I'll get something for dinner. You can bring Timmy over. We can be on your schedule, so whatever time you can fit in. It was clear that this Dorc person is looking into things related to Ernest Stanton, and I think it would be best if both of us were careful."

"Meaning I shouldn't mention you to friends or workmates?" she said.

"Well, yeah, at least for now to play it safe."

"Yes, let's meet for dinner. I'll bring it, along with Timmy. And I appreciate you being cautious. I think it's a very wise idea."

"I'll see you whenever you can make it over. Maybe give me a call when you're about to leave."

"We'll be there before 7:00," she said and disconnected.

"You're going to meet up with her tonight?" Louie asked.

"Yeah, she's coming over to my place and bringing dinner. We'll have to take a pass on The Spot tonight."

Gretchen's phone call reminded me that I was supposed to send my information to Justin Dorc. I pulled out his business card and sent him an email with my office phone number and my email address. I followed up with the 'A pleasure to meet you this afternoon' line and sent the email.

Louie headed over to The Spot, and I took Morton on a walk. As we passed by The Spot and headed for our car, Morton gave a little whine. No doubt disappointed that there wouldn't be any pork rinds tonight.

"Don't worry, Morton. I'm sure Gretchen and Timmy will bring you a treat." At the sound of Timmy's name, Morton's attitude seemed to immediately improve, and he hopped into the backseat of the car. I filled his water dish, let him out into the backyard, then hurried upstairs and straightened things out in the bedroom. I grabbed a quick shower and went up to Solo Vino, the wine store just a block away where I picked up three bottles of chilled wine.

I'd just stepped out of the store when my phone rang. "Hi Gretchen, can you still make it over tonight?"

"Yes, we're just about to head your way. If you would please turn your oven on to four-hundred degrees, we'll see you in about twenty minutes."

"Looking forward to it," I said, and she disconnected.

I figured she must have hurried home and made a meatloaf or some hot dish, and she was going to bake it at my house. That seemed positive for the possibility of her making an overnight visit. As soon as I got home, I turned on the oven, placed the wine in the refrigerator, and pulled out two dog biscuits from the cookie jar. Gretchen pulled into the driveway one minute before 7:00.

She was out of the car carrying a brown paper shopping bag as Timmy strained on the leash, attempting to charge up the steps and onto the porch. I held the door open, and Morton hurried onto the porch to greet Timmy. Gretchen reached down, unclipped the leash, and the two of them charged into the house.

"Great to see you. Thanks for coming over. How's your sanity?" I asked and got a peck on the lips in return.

"My sanity, I'll tell you, questionable at best. I'm hoping you have some wine chilling."

"You're in luck, but I'll insist that you drink out of a glass and not the bottle," I said as we made our way into the kitchen. Morton and Timmy charged past us, into the entry, and then back into the kitchen. "Let me deal with these two," I said and opened the back door. I grabbed the two dog biscuits resting on the kitchen counter and stepped outside. Morton and Timmy followed. I handed each a biscuit, and they retreated to opposite corners of the backyard. When I stepped back into the kitchen, Gretchen had already opened a wine bottle and handed me a glass. Two frozen pizzas rested on the kitchen counter.

We clinked glasses, and I said, "A tough couple of days?"

"Yes, but before I get into it, tell me about your meeting with Justin Dorc."

"Not a lot to tell other than it was strange. The information I provided was nothing unique. I answered his questions, but I just had the sense there was something else going on that he wasn't addressing. Like I told you, as I left the interview room, the officer, a detective sergeant known for not taking any bullshit, told me he was sorry for taking up my time. I've known him for a number of years, and I've never heard him say anything like that." I went on to tell her what I could recall of the questions Dorc asked.

"Vintage," she said and shook her head. "Why in the world they would have him following up on Stanton's disappearance is beyond me."

"Disappearance? Stanton is missing?"

She rolled her eyes. "Oh God, we've been dealing with this for the last few days. I'm sorry. I didn't mean to mention it, but we've done nothing but try to find him. The police department received a call on Sunday. They contacted us on Monday, and we were at his office at 10:00. We'd planned to charge him, but instead, we've been searching for him. There's no record of him taking a commercial flight. His car is missing. We've searched his house, which, by the way, appeared to be either ransacked or he lived in an absolute mess. Files and papers were scattered all over. His office was neat but missing three drawers of files. There hasn't been any activity on his five credit cards."

"Back up for a second. You said his car was missing?"

"Yes, it's an expensive—"

"An expensive Range Rover that goes for around three hundred grand."

"Oh, so you're familiar with it?"

"Not really. I've seen it. I saw it two days ago over in Mendota. I know it was his car because I had a pal at the DMV run the license plate number for me. It was parked in the driveway at Tracey Wilde's house for most of the day. The thing is a Range Rover SV Carmel edition that, like I said, goes for almost three hundred grand."

"And you're sure you saw it in Tracey Wilde's driveway?"

"Absolutely. The funny thing was that this oddball character that hangs around her place was parked on the next street over. I'm actually watching him because her soon-to-be former husband was concerned about the guy. I put a tracking device on his car so I know it was parked a block away for the better part of the day. Sometime between 4:00 in the afternoon and 8:00 at night, this oddball, his name is Davy Ruff, pulled his car into Tracey's driveway and spent the night at her place. He's a photographer by trade, but there's something about his relationship with Tracey that's a little spooky. He seems to be rather possessive regarding her, and I suspect he's getting paid for the photography he does for her with sex."

"Davy Ruff?"

"Yeah, he was following me for a while. After I told Ernest Stanton that I quit, I went to Tracey Wilde and told her I couldn't find anything negative on her husband, and I was going to shut down that investigation and send her a bill."

"How did she take that?"

"Actually, she didn't seem too surprised. She was disappointed, and I'm sure she would have loved to find a way to sue her husband for some alimony, but he wasn't cheating on her, at least that I could discover, and at the time, she was making way more money than he was."

"Oh, God, I'm sorry, Dev, but I need to make a phone call. Why don't you put those pizzas in the oven," she said as she picked up her wine glass and headed into the den.

Thirty-three

After twenty minutes I took the pizzas out of the oven. Gretchen was still in the den, talking on the phone. I grabbed the wine bottle from the refrigerator and headed into the den. She was seated on the couch, and her empty glass was on the coffee table.

"But, Jack, that's two days after he was missing. No, he did not, but still, the vehicle was there and confirmed via the license plate by someone down at the DMV," she said.

I refilled her wine glass. She nodded a thank you and took a sip.

I headed back into the kitchen. I took the pizza cutter out of the drawer, cut up the pizzas, and placed a slice of each onto a plate. I took the plate back into the den and set it on the coffee table. I placed a couple of paper napkins next to the plate and went back into the kitchen. Ten minutes later, Gretchen stepped into the kitchen with her empty plate.

"Sorry about that. You don't want to go downtown and be interviewed tonight, do you?"

"Not particularly."

"Good, because I gave your address to my boss, and he's on his way over."

"He's coming over here?"

"Yeah, I know, believe me, I know. But he's an okay guy, and once you tell him what you told me, he'll leave, and we'll have the rest of the night to relax," she said and rubbed both her hands slowly across my chest, raising her eyebrows.

"You're probably just wiping the pizza sauce off your fingers," I said.

She slapped my chest and laughed. "Oh, can I have another piece of the one with everything on it, please? I promise I'll make this up to you later tonight."

We ate the better part of both pizzas while sitting at the kitchen table. We occasionally glanced out the window to check on the dogs. They appeared to be enjoying themselves. It was almost 8:30 when the doorbell rang.

"Oh, that's probably Jack. I'll let him in and—"

"Wait here. I'll answer the door. Let's just play it safe, okay."

"You're the boss," she said.

"I am?" I replied and headed out of the kitchen as she laughed.

The guy at the door was wearing jeans and a golf shirt. I pegged him for late forties, maybe fifty. He had neatly trimmed dark hair with just a hint of some gray around the temples. As I opened the door, he said, "Mr. Haskell?"

"Yes, and you must be Jack McDonald."

"Guilty as charged," he said and held out his hand. "Thank you for letting me interrupt your evening. I don't know if Gretchen told you, but we've been dealing with a missing person report on Ernest Stanton for several days."

"Actually, she's been fairly tight-lipped about releasing any information to me."

He smiled and said, "That sounds about right."

"Come on back to the kitchen. Now, is this a formal interview, or can I offer you a glass of wine or a beer?"

"Thanks, a beer would be great."

"Hi, Jack," Gretchen said as we stepped into the kitchen. "Any problem finding the place?"

"No, I grew up not far from here, so I'm familiar with the streets."

"Can I talk you into some pizza, Jack? We've got one with about four kinds of cheese and a slice left of one with everything on it."

"Whatever you have would be wonderful," he said. I set a beer and a plate with four slices in front of him a moment later. I topped up Gretchen's glass and sat down.

Jack took a bite of pizza and said, "So, Gretchen told me you saw Ernest Stanton two days ago?"

"No, I saw his car. It was parked in the driveway at Tracey Wilde's house out in Mendota. I believe you're familiar with her."

"She appears to be the recipient of some fairly hefty investments compliments of Mr. Stanton. You were working for him?"

"I'm a Private Investigator. My name was passed on to Ernest Stanton. I was told that, if I was interested, I should contact him. I don't believe I'd ever heard of him previously. I phoned his office, and we set up a meeting. After meeting with him, I began to look into some general items for him and, in short order, decided I did not want to work for him. I went to his office and told him there was nothing I found on the individual he had me investigate, which was true. When I told him I quit, he went ballistic, literally screaming and swearing at me in his office. I tried to remain polite and told him I would not be sending him a bill. I left his office. As I departed, he continued to scream at me. I have not heard nor actually seen him since that day."

"But you did see his vehicle."

"Yes, I did." I went on to tell him about the vehicle parked for hours in Tracey's driveway and about Ruff's car parked a block away. "One other thing comes to mind. As I'm driving toward Tracey's house, I can see her fire pit on the back patio. There were flames two or three feet high in the fire pit. It was a hot, humid day, early afternoon, and she had the fire pit burning. I was more interested in the Range Rover parked in her driveway and forgot about it until now. But now I'm wondering if maybe she was burning items. You know, files or receipts, that sort of thing."

McDonald seemed to think for a moment, shot a look at Gretchen, and said, "I've seen her house. There's plenty of room to park on the street. Was there something going on and a lot of cars parked out on the street?"

"No, nothing like that. I placed a tracking device on Ruff's car and knew the car was a block away. The lots in that area are large, usually one or two acres. Ruff's car was parked between two lots, which suggested to me that he wasn't seeing anyone in either house. He could have taken a shortcut and walked across their back lawns and over to Tracey's house, but I didn't think he'd do that. Ruff wasn't in the car when I checked it, and I never actually saw him. My guess would be he was somewhere in Tracey's house, but that's just a guess. I never actually got out of my car and really have no idea where Ruff was. I just found it strange that his car was essentially hidden on the next street."

"Are you familiar with this Ruff person?"

"Yes and no. I don't know him personally. I'm keeping an eye on him for a client. A man by the name of Percy Riggs, he's in the midst of divorce proceedings with Tracey Wilde. Tracey had hired me to investigate Percy, hoping to discover an affair. I never found anything remotely pointing to that sort activity. I brought my investigation to a close, told her I couldn't find anything on her husband, and ended my investigation the day after I quit working for Ernest Stanton. Another investigator I know was working for Percy Riggs. Riggs was concerned about Ruff harming his two employees or doing something that might affect his tech business. He hired me to essentially keep an eye on Ruff, which I'm still doing."

"Good lord, talk about a small town," McDonald said and picked up another slice of pizza from the plate in front of him.

"Saint Small. I often tell folks St. Paul is the largest small town in the country," I said, which got a laugh from both McDonald and Gretchen. "Do you have any idea where Ernest Stanton might be?"

McDonald shook his head. "I understand you had the pleasure of discussing this with a state investigator."

"You mean Justin Dorc? Aptly named, although the spelling is incorrect. Yeah, I was called down to the St. Paul Police Station. To be honest, he asked some pretty general questions. It was almost as if he hadn't reviewed the file on Stanton. I answered his questions and left after about twenty minutes. On my way out, the Detective Sergeant who was in the room with Dorc patted me on the shoulder when I left and apologized for taking up my time."

"It never ends," McDonald said and shook his head. We discussed general things over the next half-hour, and then he left. I refilled Gretchen's wine glass and brought Morton and Timmy into the house. Gretchen took a couple of sips from her glass then said they should head home.

I was about to protest but, on second thought, decided not to. I walked them out to her car, thanked her for coming over, and watched as she drove off. No kiss, no wave, no toot of the horn.

Thirty-four

I could say I watched the 10:00 news, but the truth was, I had it on and wasn't paying attention. Instead, I was wondering what I'd said or done that made Gretchen decide to leave. Everything seemed to be going well. I think Jack McDonald left on a positive note. I'd been lying awake in bed for the past forty-five minutes when my phone alerted me to Davy Ruff's Chevy Spark on the move. I grabbed my cell phone off the bedside table and turned it on. The car was just heading up the block from Ruff's house and turning at the corner. I turned the phone off, thought for a moment, and then climbed out of bed.

Between Gretchen heading back to her house and Ruff on the move, there was no way I was going to fall asleep. I got dressed and went downstairs. There was one slice of pizza left on a plate in the refrigerator. I took it out and ate it, then turned on my cell phone. Ruff was just pulling onto 35E and heading south. Did I really need to follow him out to Tracey's? It was no more than a half-second before I grabbed my car keys and hurried out to the garage.

I backed out of the driveway and headed down Selby Avenue. I took a right onto Western Ave and, from there, headed down Ramsey Hill and onto the entrance to 35E. There was no one behind me at this hour. I pulled to the side and turned on my cell phone. Ruff was still a couple of miles from my location. I watched on my phone as his car gradually approached. I turned off my phone and pulled onto the highway as he drove past. I sped up, heading for the tail lights that I hoped were his. Luckily, the tail lights were on an ugly pea-green Chevy Spark. I turned into the righthand lane because I knew Ruff would take the Mendota exit on the far side of the river bridge, only he didn't and kept heading south on 35E. I followed him for the next twenty minutes until he finally took the exit for 185th street and headed west. I followed him through a number of recent housing divisions and the occasional cornfield until he turned onto Eagle Creek Avenue in the town of Prior Lake. We crossed a bridge between upper and lower Prior Lake, and he took the next left, pulling into an area of very large and, I presumed, very expensive lake homes.

It was almost 1:00 in the morning. The street was wide and curved along the shore of the lake. There weren't any street lights, but I could still see with my headlights turned off and followed Ruff around a bend in the road. He suddenly pulled into the driveway of a large two-story brick mansion. As he pulled into the driveway, one of the three attached garage doors rose.

He drove into the garage, and the door closed behind him.

The mailbox for the mansion was on a wooden post at the curb. I quickly pulled over to the mailbox, read the address, 15651, and drove down the street. I stopped three doors down and parked. I wrote down the address and looked around. At this hour, most of the homes were dark. Only a couple had a porch light on. One of the benefits of living in the burbs or a small town, I guessed, was that crime apparently wasn't quite as rampant.

I climbed out of my car and walked back to the structure Ruff had entered. The place was still dark. I waited next to a large tree in the yard, but the place remained dark. There wasn't a light on anywhere in the house that I could see. I walked along the side of the house toward the lake. I was still unable to see any lights on anywhere in the house. The front of the structure faced the lake. There was a dock and a boathouse down by the shore, and I could detect a large boat raised up over the water. A staircase led down from the house to a brick patio with a fireplace at one end and a grill beneath a cover. There was a metal table with eight chairs and, beyond that, three metal couches with flowered cushions surrounding what I guessed would be a gas fire pit. I studied the house for a couple of minutes, but the lights remained off.

Suddenly, there was a light, for just a brief moment, and then it reappeared, a flashlight. It had to be Ruff carrying the flashlight. It didn't light up the room with the large picture window, but it did illuminate Ruff's legs as he carried the flashlight for three or four seconds hurrying across the room. I moved toward the lake and then turned around to study the house. None of the rooms were illuminated, but if the shades had been drawn and the drapes had been pulled, I wouldn't be able to see any light.

It seemed fairly obvious to me that Ruff was probably the only person in the place. Did he know who lived there? Was he robbing the place? I stood and waited for something, anything, to happen. I hoped for another illumination from the flashlight or maybe a TV screen lighting up the room with the picture window, but nothing happened.

I was beginning to be discovered by the mosquitoes. At first, it was just one or two. That quickly changed to a number of them whining around my ears. I was now moving my arms constantly, and they were still settling on and attacking me. I was swatting them away from my face, but there just seemed to be more and more of them.

They were finding a way through my jeans and attacking my thighs. All the while letting off that high-pitch whine. I finally had to flee the scene and get back to the safety of my car. I hurried along the side of the house, then stopped at the corner and peeked around to make sure no one was looking. The garage door Ruff had opened was still closed. I was afraid if I waited any longer, I'd need a transfusion from all the blood the mosquitoes had sucked out of me. I hurried out to the street and glanced around. I couldn't see anyone watching me, and I opened the mailbox. There was a stack of envelopes, and I grabbed them and ran to my car. I slid in behind the wheel and quietly closed the door. At least a half-dozen mosquitoes followed me into the car. I held out my bare arm, now covered with swollen bites. As the mosquitoes landed, I slapped at them, payback for the attack. Finally, the car was quiet. I waited for a few minutes, but nothing happened, so I turned on my car and drove my wounded body back home.

I pulled into my garage and entered through the back door. My entrance was mosquito free. I set the envelopes I'd taken on the kitchen table and glanced at the top one. It was addressed to Mr. Ernest Stanton at 15651 Highland Avenue Northwest, Prior Lake, Minnesota.

Ruff was going through Stanton's house. That presented a number of questions, like how and why? He obviously had a garage door opener and probably keys to the place. So, where was Stanton? What happened to him? Where was his fancy Range Rover? I thought about calling Gretchen, but it was almost 2:00 in the morning. I only had an office number for Jack McDonald. I called the number and left a message. "Hi, Jack, Dev Haskell. Davy Ruff is in the process of going through Ernest Stanton's home out in Prior Lake. Give me a call when you get this." I left Stanton's address along with my number.

I looked at my arms. There were at least twenty red, swollen mosquito bites on each arm. I was suddenly tired. No, let me rephrase that. I was exhausted. I went upstairs. Morton had climbed up onto my bed and was now stretched out and sound asleep. I undressed, headed into the bathroom, and glanced in the mirror. I looked like a teenager with pimples. Only they were mosquito bites. I turned on the shower and stepped in. It felt wonderful, and I lathered up twice and stood under the stream of water for a good twenty minutes.

I headed back into the bedroom. Morton was still stretched out and hadn't moved. He had left just enough room for me if I slept on my side. I closed my eyes, and the next thing I knew, my alarm was going off.

Thirty-five

Sitting on the edge of my bed and turned on my cell phone to see where Davy Ruff's car was. It was parked next to his house. I guessed that since he'd been in Stanton's house until the wee hours of this morning, he'd gone back home from there rather than spend the night at Tracey's.

I'd been downstairs for almost an hour before Morton wandered in. I gave him a head scratch and let him out into the backyard. The mosquito bites on my arms and face were still swollen and pink. I went upstairs to the bathroom and rubbed Benadryl over the bites to hopefully reduce the swelling and the pink color. Once Morton had been fed, we headed down to the office.

It was a little after 8:00, and I left another phone message for Jack McDonald. He returned my call a half-hour later. "Good morning, Dev. I saw your messages. What can I do for you?"

"Did you listen to them?"

"No, that's why I'm calling now. What's up?"

I told him about Davy Ruff going into Stanton's house late last night.

"Did you call the police?"

"No, I thought it might be better to see what he took. He certainly had access to the place. He had a garage door opener and was inside the house using a flashlight. That suggests to me he didn't want any neighbors to be aware he was in the place. Quite possibly, he had keys to the house. I thought you would be able to obtain a warrant without any problem and could check out Ruff's home this morning. You mentioned yesterday that files were missing from Stanton's place. I would say there's a pretty good chance they would be in Ruff's house or possibly Tracey Wilde's home."

McDonald seemed to think about that for a moment and said, "Let me get back to you," and hung up.

I decided it would be a good idea to call Gretchen and keep her appraised. I ended up leaving a message. "Hi Gretchen, Dev calling. Please give me a call. I just got off the phone with Jack McDonald," I said and gave her a two-sentence update.

My phone rang three minutes later. Gretchen returning my call. "Dev, Davy Ruff was in Ernest Stanton's home? Did you call the police?"

"Good morning, Gretchen. Ruff was in there late last night, actually early this morning. I followed him out there." I went on to tell her about the garage door opener and Ruff going through the house with a flashlight.

"Why didn't you call the police?"

"Because if Ernest Stanton is still alive and Ruff is working with someone else, Ruff's arrest could very well lead to Stanton's death."

"But if he was arrested, how would he be able to kill Stanton?"

"Gretchen, listen to me. If Ruff has a partner, say, for instance, Tracey Wilde, if Ruff is arrested, she, or whoever might be in on the deal, would probably kill Stanton and dispose of the body. Pretty tough to prove kidnapping, let alone murder, at that point."

"You said you spoke to Jack McDonald?"

"Yes, just a couple of minutes ago."

"What is he going to do?"

"I don't know, exactly. He told me he would be in touch and got off the phone."

"I suspect I'll hear from him at some point and—Oh, this is him calling me now. I'd better take this," she said and hung up.

Just in case, I checked Davy Ruff's car. It was still parked next to his house. I was debating calling Tracey back when Louie stepped into the office. I'd been so focused on interacting with the State Attorney General's office I hadn't heard him groan his way up the staircase. He gave me a wave as he headed toward his desk chair. I filled his coffee mug as he sat down and set it in front of him. He nodded a thank you and took a sip. I topped up my mug, sat down, and checked Ruff's car again. It was still next to his house.

Louie stared at me for the next few minutes before he asked, "Do you have measles or some weird food allergy? What are all those spots from?"

"I was attacked by a couple thousand mosquitoes. Nothing short of crazy if you want the truth." I gave him the update on meeting Jack McDonald and my midnight run following Davy Ruff to Stanton's house.

"So, are they doing anything about Ruff going through the house?"

"I'm not sure," I explained why I didn't call the police. "I don't really know what they can do right now. My word on Ruff's activities last night isn't grounds for an arrest. I suppose they could go into Stanton's house, but I'm not sure they would be able to identify something as missing. A number of files had already been taken. Maybe everything Ruff or Tracey wanted was already out of there. I think they may have been burning files or receipts in the fire pit at Tracey's, and I told McDonald that. It could be Ruff was just pulling off a standard burglary, taking jewelry, cash, and some valuable items. Who knows?"

"The whole thing sounds crazy," Louie said and shook his head. "You got a porn star, her photographer, and this investment guru. Honest to god, you can't make it up."

"Yeah, Louie, it's hard to believe, but all of a sudden, you and I are looking pretty good."

"Not to worry, Dev, that will change."

It was toward the end of the afternoon when my desk phone rang. "Haskell Investigations."

"Good afternoon, Dev. Apparently, your receptionist took a late lunch."

"Hi, Aaron. Don't tell me someone else has accused me of some major crime, and you want me down there."

"Half-right, I thought you might find this interesting. We were contacted this morning by Jack McDonald. He's with the State Attorney General's Office. Apparently, you gave him a lead on an individual by the name—"

"It wouldn't happen to be Davy Ruff, would it? He's a photographer who has been working with Tracey Wilde. A bit of a character. I saw him break into Ernest Stanton's house around midnight last night."

"That's what we've been told. McDonald and Manning are going to be interviewing Ruff in another half-hour. I thought you might be interested in a seat in the viewing room. You might have some suggestions or feedback as they conduct the interview. Sounds like you're familiar with the circumstances."

"You're referring to his going through Ernest Stanton's home out in Prior Lake?"

"Yes, along with his relationship with Miss Wilde."

"Have you spoken with her, Tracey Wilde?"

"She's lawyered up. We're hoping some pressure on Ruff might give us enough information to bring her in."

"You said a half-hour?"

"That's right."

"I'll head out now. Thanks for the call," I said and hung up.

Louie looked up from the file he was reading. "They want to talk to you again? I can go down there with you and—"

"Thanks, Louie, but I'm okay. They brought in Davy Ruff. Aaron asked me to sit in the viewing room and see if I come up with any ideas."

"So they're not going to charge you?"

"That's what it sounds like. If they start heading down that path, I'll clam up and give you a call. I'm not sure how long this is going to last, so I think I'll take Morton home and—"

"I can take him over to The Spot, and when you're finished, you can join us."

"Thanks, but there's a chance this could go into the late hours, so I think I better take him home."

"Okay, good luck, and if you get a sense they're giving you the evil eye, give me a call right away."

"Thanks, Louie. I'll do that. Hey, Morton, come on, let's go for a ride," I said.

Morton hopped off his pillow and stood with his nose next to the door. His tail continuously slapped against the wall. I clipped the leash onto his collar, and we headed downstairs and out the door. We drove home, pulled into the driveway, and I took him on a walk around the block. Once in the house, he settled onto his pillow in the kitchen and got close up and personal with his rawhide bone. I headed down to the police station and asked for Aaron LaZelle at the front desk.

Five minutes later, a uniformed officer opened the security door and called my name. I hurried over to him, and we headed down the hall to the elevators. I hadn't met him before, but I noticed his uniform shirt had the name McGinn embroidered above the pocket. "Would your father happen to be Ed McGinn?" I asked as we stepped onto the elevator.

He smiled and said, "Yeah, that's my dad. He's mentioned you once or twice."

"Well, don't believe what he says. I'm really a very nice guy."

He laughed and said, "Actually, that's what he tells me. They're going to be in Interview Room Two. I'm going to take you into the viewing room. Lieutenant LaZelle will be joining you at some point. I don't know if anyone else will be in there with you."

When we stepped into the viewing room, it was empty. I settled into a chair in the front row. The room was like a small theatre with three rows of comfortable, upholstered chairs, four chairs to a row, for a total of a dozen chairs. Each row was slightly higher than the one in front of it. At the moment, no one was in the interview room.

"Can I get you a coffee or a tea?" McGinn asked.

"No, thanks, but I'm good. Please say hi to your dad for me when you see him."

He nodded and said, "I'll be sure to do that." As he stepped out of the viewing room, the door opened on the interview room, and Davy Ruff was escorted in.

Thirty-six

R uff wasn't in handcuffs, which made me wonder if he had even been arrested or if he came down here of his own free will. The officer that escorted him in directed him to a chair on the far side of the metal table, which meant that he would essentially be facing me during the entire process, although he couldn't see me and, I presumed, had no idea I was watching.

"Mr. Ruff, can I get you a coffee or a soda?" the escorting officer asked.

Ruff shook his head and said, "No thanks."

"Detective Manning and Mr. McDonald will be with you in just a moment," the officer said and left the room. Ruff glanced around the room. He studied the four-wheel cart loaded with the recording equipment. The camera mounted on the wall was just above the windows that I was looking through, so I couldn't tell if the camera was on. He examined the steel table with the attachments for handcuffs and leg restraints. I had the distinct feeling this was probably his first time in an interview room.

All of a sudden, the door opened, and Detective Sergeant Manning stepped into the room, followed by Jack McDonald. Manning was carrying a thick file folder, and I wondered if it was filled with documents related to Ernest Stanton or if it was just stuffed with papers meant to add some pressure on Ruff.

"Mr. Ruff, sorry to keep you waiting. Thank you for your patience. I'm Detective Norris Manning, and this is Jack McDonald. He's with the state," Manning said and gave a nod to Ruff.

McDonald stepped over, nodded, and said, "Nice to meet you."

"Before we get started, can I get you a coffee or maybe a water or something?" Manning asked.

Ruff shook his head and joked, "I'd love a beer right about now."

"Wouldn't we all," Manning said and gave an evil chuckle as he pulled out a chair and sat down. McDonald did the same. Once they were settled in, Manning opened the file and lifted the top sheet. He seemed to read it for maybe ten seconds. While he did so, Ruff nervously licked his lips a half-dozen times.

The door to the viewing room opened, and Aaron stepped in. I gave him a wave. As he settled into a chair, I said, "Nice timing. I think it's about to get interesting."

"Well, I'd better follow the rules here," Manning said and stared at Ruff for a long moment. Ruff seemed to shift uncomfortably, and Manning began to read Ruff his rights.

Ruff's eyes grew wide, and he slowly shook his head. I thought he may have mouthed the 'F' word two or three times, but I couldn't be sure. Suddenly, it was very obvious he didn't look happy.

As Manning finished, Ruff said, "I don't need a lawyer 'cause I didn't do anything wrong."

Manning nodded and said, "Very well. So, Mr. Ruff. Let me ask you, are you familiar with a man by the name of Ernest Stanton?"

Ruff seemed to think for a long moment and then shook his head. "No, never heard of him."

"Oh, interesting. The reason I mention that is because it would appear you were involved early this morning in a break-in out in Prior Lake. Since we have a case concerning an individual who has been missing for a number of days and seeing as how you apparently had access to his home, I would like you to explain exactly how you obtained access and where the individual might be at the moment."

Ruff shook his head and said, "I'm afraid you got the wrong guy. I was home asleep last night. I was tired and went to bed just a little after 9:00. I slept through the night and didn't wake up until you guys knocked on my door this morning."

"So you're saying you slept from around 9:00 last night until almost noon today?"

Ruff seemed to think about that for a moment and then nodded. "Yeah, I was really beat."

"Did you loan your car to anyone?" Manning asked.

Ruff shook his head and said, "No, I did not."

"I see. Can you explain how this image from a security camera came to be?" Manning asked as he pulled an image from the file and handed it to Ruff. "You'll note that it has today's date and a time of 0:53 AM. That's seven minutes before one o'clock in the morning, and that certainly appears to be your car, a Chevrolet Spark. I believe it's a 2015, if I'm not mistaken. Now, you were found guilty last year of driving under the influence, which is why your car has that special license plate that is displayed in the picture. So let me ask again, how did you gain access to the home? How did the garage door rise up so you could park in the garage and then walk through the house with a flashlight?"

"That wasn't me. I don't know how any of that happened. I already told both of you I was asleep at home, and I—"

"Mr. Ruff, you are now at that critical part of our discussion where we have presented you with the facts. We have you on security tape driving in and parking in one of Ernest Stanton's garages. We have an eyewitness who watched as you walked through Mr. Stanton's home with a flashlight. We have evidence that suggests you left the Stanton residence early this morning in possession of a sterling silver flatware service. More importantly, Ernest Stanton has been missing for five days now, and you suddenly have access to his house. Think carefully about your response."

"I'm pretty sure he flew out to Hawaii or some-place."

"Unfortunately, Mr. Ruff, we've checked with all the airlines. Mr. Stanton never boarded a plane. He never passed through a TSA checkpoint. The Transportation Security Administration has no record of Ernest Stanton flying anywhere for the last two months. I guess what I'm suggesting is that it would be in your best interest to tell the truth. Give us the information you have, and we can work out a deal for you that will reduce the time you're going to be spending behind bars. And believe me, as it stands now, you are going to end up behind bars."

"But I told you guys before. I don't know anything. Besides, Stanton told me he never used the silverware, and so I could have it."

"That's interesting, Mr. Ruff. Because just a moment earlier, you told us you'd never heard of Ernest Stanton."

"Okay, okay, just hold on. I didn't kidnap the guy, if that's what you're thinking, okay? You gotta believe me. I went over there and got a bunch of files and stuff, and we, I mean Tracey and Stanton, they set them on fire and burned shit for like a day-and-a-half. He showed up at Tracey's four or five days ago, and he's this kinky kind of guy. She's got a dungeon down in her basement. It's a soundproof room with all sorts of leather and chains and stuff. Stanton wanted Tracey to lock him up in there. He wanted her to play all that bondage and dis-cipline stuff with him, and I think one thing led to an-other, and she maybe kind of took total control of the dude."

"You mean she killed him?"

"No, I didn't mean that. As far as I know, he's still chained to the bed with a smile on his face. He's wearing a leather mask and stuff, and he's paying her a bunch of dough to let him stay there for a while. Then he's going to move to someplace in the far east. I don't know, Thai-land, or China, or someplace like that. It's kind of like he's in hiding and at the same time enjoying himself, ex-cept I've never been into that stuff."

"So, as far as you know, he's in a room in the base-ment of her home?"

"Yeah, and it's not like she kidnapped him or any-thing. He's digging it. He's hiding in there. She brings him three meals a day. Keeps him chained to the bed, and he thinks that's cool, and then a couple of times a day, well, he gets some, how should I say, some addi-tional service."

"So, would it be safe to say he's hiding in this room?" Manning asked.

Ruff shook his head. "No, he's not hiding. Tracey knows he's there. She probably spends half a day in there, not all at once, but you know, bringing him meals and umm, how can I say, umm, fulfilling his needs, I guess."

I glanced over at Aaron, who was smiling and shaking his head.

Thirty-seven

The interview continued for another hour. Ruff provided more of the same information. Not the least of which was that Stanton sold his car, the Range Rover SC Carmel edition, to some collector down in Chicago. The car had been in Tracey's garage and was loaded onto a truck two days ago and hauled down to Chicago. By the end of the interview, both Manning and McDonald, along with Aaron LaZelle, decided not to arrest Ruff but to hold him for a few more hours. It was after 7:00, and they were discussing the benefits of waiting until morning before arresting Stanton or, if they did arrest him, what, exactly, the charges would be.

McDonald was on the line with financial and legal people at the state, and finally, the decision was made to release Ruff and place two state agents outside Tracey's home in the event Stanton tried to leave.

There seemed to be a plan afoot, but no one was telling me anything, so I went home. The following morning, Morton and I had just arrived at the office when my cell phone rang. "Hi, Gretchen. What's up? Were you going to do a walk this morning?"

"No time for that, unfortunately, Dev. We just received word. The Stanton Investment Firms' bank accounts have been drained."

"Drained, by who? When?"

"By Ernest Stanton. Apparently, this was set up two weeks ago."

"Two weeks ago, and no one in your office knew about it?"

"It was scheduled two weeks ago to drain the accounts last night. The call came through first thing this morning from one of the accountants in the firm. There are no funds to cover paychecks or any bills."

I didn't respond for a long moment. Finally, I said, "I can't believe this. I'm not a finance guy, but that doesn't just happen. There had to be some serious planning on this."

"You're right, and unfortunately, no one was aware of it."

"Well, if the funds were transferred, they had to end up somewhere. Where did they go?"

"Outside the country. It appears they've gone from one place to another. We're attempting to track them and running into a number of problems. They went from Switzerland to Singapore and, I'm sure, a dozen locations after that. We've yet to hear anything from Singapore, and we'll have to wait another day at this point."

"Is Jack McDonald aware of this?"

"He's been on the phone since we were informed, and it's not going well."

"Do you know if he contacted the St. Paul Police?"

"I'm sorry, I don't know. That's why I called to see if you could get in touch. I know you watched the interview of this Ruff character. I just don't know what to tell you."

"I'll call St. Paul now. Bye," I said and hung up. I phoned Aaron LaZelle and crossed my fingers. "Dev," he answered just after the first ring.

"Aaron, I just got a call from someone at state. They said—"

"We're en route to Tracey Wilde's now. I just hope Stanton is still there."

"Didn't you have two people out there keeping an eye on the place?"

"No, they were, or rather are, state agents, but they couldn't enter the house. I've got a warrant that will get us in. I just hope Stanton is still there. We're just pulling off of the 35E bridge now. I better go," Aaron said and disconnected.

I opened my desk drawer, tossed Morton a biscuit, and hurried out the door. Just as I crossed the street, Louie's faded Ford Fiesta pulled in behind my car. "You off somewhere?" Louie asked as he climbed out of his car.

"Yeah, a major screw-up on this Stanton deal. Apparently, someone, probably Stanton, drained the company's bank accounts. God, it could be millions," I said. "Anyway, they just found out this morning when they went to transfer funds for paychecks. Aaron is on his way to Tracey Wilde's, so I'm going to head out there."

"Where's Stanton? Is he out at Tracey's?"

"That's the million-dollar question, Louie." I slid behind the wheel, put the car in gear, and sped up the street. I turned onto 35E and floored it, racing past cars crossing the bridge. I took the exit off the bridge and drove up the ramp to Highway 13. The light at the intersection was red. No one was in front of me. I let two cars pass, ran the red light, pulled onto Highway 13, and sped toward Tracey's development. As I rounded the corner to her house, I counted five cars. A Mendota squad car was pulled across the entrance to the driveway. Two St. Paul squad cars were parked behind it. Two more unmarked cars were parked at odd angles, I guessed one might be the state car that was here overnight, and I had no idea who had been in the other vehicle.

I parked behind one of the St. Paul squad cars and hurried across the lawn to the front door. No one was minding the door, so I stepped inside. I hurried through the living room, past the fireplace with the painting of Tracey, and into the kitchen. I spotted Tracey out on the patio. At the moment, she was seated at the table with Detective Manning and Jack McDonald. Manning appeared to be asking a series of questions. Tracey was shaking her head and not looking very happy. Off to the side, a guy in a one-piece disposable suit, latex gloves, and a disposable mask was sifting through the ashes in the fire pit.

I suddenly heard an angry voice from behind a door I hadn't noticed the last time I was in the kitchen. I opened the door, and the voice became louder as it rose up the staircase. "Apparently, you are incapable of listening or understanding. I'll have you know, I'm the CEO, the Chief Executive Officer of Rebel Investments. I am not in hiding. I'm on a retreat to focus on my next business move. There is nothing illegal about what I am doing at the moment."

I hurried down the stairs, trying not to make any noise. I entered a large dim room illuminated by two basement windows and an open door at the far end with light spilling out. I headed for the open door.

"I'll have you know I started my business over thirty years ago. I built it from the ground up into the successful enterprise that it is today, and I—"

"The bank accounts for your successful enterprise have been drained. Your home in Prior Lake was listed for sale twenty-four hours ago, and you appear to be hiding in this dungeon room in the basement." I recognized Aaron's voice.

"I happen to be a major investor in the studio that operates out of this facility. If you'd care to check with Miss Wilde, I'm sure—"

"We have a team talking to her now," Aaron said just as I stepped into the room.

I was about to say something. God knows what. But at the moment, I was literally stunned. Aaron stood between two uniformed officers, one from St. Paul and the other from Mendota. All three were wearing latex gloves.

Ernest Stanton stood facing them. At least, I thought the individual was Ernest Stanton. At the moment, he was wearing a black leather hood that covered most of his face, down to the tip of his nose. It was the only thing he was wearing, well, other than a black leather thong. Although, that was hard to see because his massive belly hung down over the thong. I did note that there were two leather straps wrapped around each fat, hairy thigh with a small padlock attached. The dimples in his thighs and the 'love handles' that draped over the leather thong made it look like Stanton had suffered from hail damage.

"Dev? How did you get in?" Aaron asked.

"I let myself in."

"Don't tell me this is where you're getting your information. Perfect, wonderful. I'm going to sue your department, officer, and as for you, Haskell, I told you before. You're fired!"

"Actually, I told you I quit, that I didn't like working for you, and I wasn't going to charge you. But I've changed my mind. I am going to charge you. I'll send you a bill while your fat ass is in jail."

"Go ahead, and good luck because there's no money in any of the accounts, and I'm going to—No, wait, I didn't mean that," he said and looked at Aaron. "You can't record that. I didn't mean to say that."

"You gave me permission, Mr. Stanton. Consider yourself under arrest," Aaron said and raised the cell phone in his hand. "You have the right to remain silent. Anything you say can and will be used against you."

"No, wait, wait. Don't do this. I can make it worth your while. I'm the Chief Executive Officer of Rebel Investments," Stanton shouted.

"Yes, and now you're under arrest. Better cuff him before you take him out," Aaron said.

The two officers looked at one another, each hoping the other would step forward. Finally, the St. Paul officer stepped forward and slapped a pair of handcuffs on Stanton's wrists. The Mendota officer stepped behind Stanton and unhooked the ten-foot chain that was attached to the king-sized bed. I'd been so focused on Stanton that, for the first time, I noticed the chains and leather straps attached to the headboard.

Once the chain was unhooked from Stanton's leather thong, Aaron nodded toward the door and said, "Get him out of here."

The officers led him out of the room and up the stairs. All the while, Stanton continued to proclaim his innocence. Halfway up the stairs, he began to promise to return the funds to the Investment accounts.

"What in God's name was that about? He's been in here chained to a bed for five days?" I asked.

"Apparently," Aaron said. "I would guess, at this point, he's not playing with a full deck. Fortunately, the officers had their body cameras on. Otherwise, no one would believe this."

Epilogue

As it turned out, Aaron found Stanton's suitcase stored beneath the bed in the dungeon and opened it to get some clothes for him. The suitcase was filled with bundles of hundred-dollar bills. Ernest Stanton was transferred from the police station to a mental health facility the following day. He's in the process of being sued by his employees as he undergoes a mental evaluation. Last I heard, he was confined to a room with padded walls and was wearing a hospital gown.

As for Tracey, she's under investigation by the state. The bank account for Bad Girl Lovers has been locked down until the state can determine how and why, exactly, three point five million dollars had been transferred into it by Rebel Investments at 2:00 AM. Tracey's soon-to-be former husband, Percy, landed the new client. He hired twenty-five computer geeks around the country and placed Luther Harris on permanent staff. He also hired a firm to proceed with the divorce proceedings that Tracey had put on hold.

Morton and I went on a few more walks with Gretchen and Timmy, but on each walk, I could tell our conversations were growing more distant. She invited us over to dinner the following Monday, and I had hopes that we might be getting back to whatever our 'normal' had been. That went out the window the moment we pulled up in front of her house, and I saw the For Sale sign.

The two of them, Gretchen and Timmy, were in the front yard. Gretchen was watering the flower boxes hanging in front of the windows, and Timmy was stretched out on the front steps. He raised his head as we pulled up and then jumped off the steps and charged toward the back door of the car, where Morton was barking out the window.

I climbed out of the car and let Morton out of the backseat. The two of them chased one another back and forth across the front yard until Gretchen got to the side gate and opened it. They charged into the backyard, and she closed the gate behind them.

I grabbed the bag with the wine bottles from the front passenger seat and then asked, "What's with the 'For Sale' sign? You've got a lovely neighborhood right here."

She nodded and said, "Well, the good news is I'm getting a promotion. The bad news is I'm being transferred up to our office in Bemidji."

"Bemidji? But that's two hundred miles north of here."

"Actually, it's two hundred and twenty-five miles north of here, but it is a promotion, and I have to take it, or I'm off future promotion lists. It's only going to be three or maybe four years. The next promotion will have me back down here, or Austin, or maybe Rochester."

"When are you leaving?"

"Well, not tonight if that's what you're worried about. I'm up in Bemidji the day after tomorrow until the end of the week. But enough of that. Come on in. I've got dinner in the oven and chilled wine ready to open. We can put your bottles in the fridge. Then, depending on your schedule, I have a bottle of breakfast champagne and maple syrup for French toast if you'd care to spend the night."

"Yes, I'd like that a lot."

"Me too," she said.

We had a wonderful dinner and chat and an exhausting late night. Gretchen served up the French toast and the breakfast champagne in bed. Morton and I got a wonderful kiss on the way out the door after breakfast, and we promised one another we would stay in touch.

I drove home, hit the shower, and headed down to the office just after twelve.

Louie wasn't back until late in the afternoon. "Oh, so you finally decided to make it in. Everything okay?" he asked.

I told him about Gretchen's promotion and her move.

"You got plans for tonight?" Louie asked.

I shook my head. "No, to tell you the truth, after the last couple of weeks, I just want to get back to being my boring old self. With Gretchen moving out of town, that shouldn't be too difficult."

"Sorry to hear about the move. I know you two were maybe heading toward being an item. Why don't you let me buy you a beer over at The Spot and get you started back to getting in trouble."

"You know, Louie, that sounds like a great plan. Hey, Morton, want to go to The Spot?"

He was off his pillow and standing with his nose to the door and his tail wagging.

"Wow, you really have him trained well," Louie said, and we both laughed.

I clipped the leash onto Morton's collar, and we headed out of the office. We crossed the street with Louie leading the way. Just as we stepped onto the sidewalk and Louie opened the front door to The Spot, a black Cadillac Escalade pulled to the curb and tooted the horn. We all turned to look as the passenger window lowered, and Fat Freddy Zimmerman said, "Tub—err—Mr. Gustafson would like to see you now, Haskell."

"Oh, come on, Freddy, can't I at least have a—"

"Now, Haskell, get in the damn car," he shouted as a muscular thug slid out of the backseat and held the door for me.

"I got Morton," Louie said and grabbed the leash from me. He and Morton stepped into The Spot.

I looked at Fat Freddy, shook my head, and thought, *'Back to getting in trouble. That was fast.'*

The End

Thank you for taking the time to read <u>Rebel Without A Clue</u>. If you enjoyed the read please consider leaving a review, even if it's just a sentence or two it really, really helps. Thank you!

Don't miss the sample of <u>Retirement Scheme</u>, a Jack Dillon Dublin Tale on the following page.

Sneak Peek

Retirement Scheme

Second Edition

MIKE FARICY

Prologue

AIB, Allied Irish Banks, is one of the big four commercial banks in Ireland, with over a hundred and seventy branches in the Republic. The Grand Canal Dock Branch is located at 2 Hanover Quay, between the South Dock Steak House and a bar called Boojum, a Mexican Burrito Bar. At 3:54 on Friday afternoon, the bank was due to close in six minutes. Two men approached the bank from opposite directions. Both men wore faded caps, disposable face masks, wigs, and latex gloves beneath their dark brown cotton gloves.

The older of the two held the door for his partner. The partner nodded and whispered, "Four minutes," as he stepped inside and headed toward the bank's teller counter. The older man stepped over to the table in the center of the lobby. A rack filled with blank deposit and withdrawal slips was in the center of the table. He stood with his back to the teller counter, facing the desks of two bank officers.

The older woman in front of the man at the teller's window thanked the teller, arranged her cash in her billfold, set the billfold in a pocket of her purse, zipped the purse closed, thanked the teller again, and stepped to the side.

The man took a deep breath, stepped forward, and said, "I'd like to make a withdrawal." He handed the bank teller his note and a shopping bag. The note read, 'Empty your drawer. I have a gun.' In case the teller had any questions, he pulled back his windbreaker, revealing the pistol in his belt. Her eyes grew wide, and he politely said, "Do it now, please."

She nodded and began to quickly pull the stacks of euro notes from her cash drawer. As she did so, the teller four feet to the left, a woman named Tierney, asked, "Megan, what are you doing? Megan?" She glanced over at Tierney.

"Megan, give her the shopping bag. Fill it up, be quiet, and nothing will happen," the robber said.

"What do you think—" She stopped and stared as he pulled back his windbreaker.

"Better just do it," Megan said. She quickly handed the shopping bag over to Tierney just as an elderly woman stepped up to the counter and slid a deposit slip and two twenty euro notes toward the teller.

"Pardon me, ma'am, I was just finishing a transaction here," the robber said as he stepped over and gently moved her aside.

"Excuse me. I think you might want to consider waiting your turn. Good heavens, where did you learn your manners?" She made a move to step back in place, but he held his ground and gave her a not-so-gentle shove. "Oh, what in the name of—"

The man at the table pulled a pistol out, fired toward the ceiling, and shouted, "Everyone on the floor, now. Come on, move, get down on the floor. Don't even think of pressing a button, you stupid slapper. Move away from your desk and get down on the floor. Everyone follows directions, and no one gets hurt. Let's go, do it now," he shouted and waved his pistol at a wide-eyed woman still seated at her desk staring at him. She suddenly moved from her chair and onto the floor. "Face down on the floor. Move. Now."

The robber reached over the teller counter, took hold of the shopping bag, glanced around for any additional currency, and headed for the door. He nodded as he passed his partner, who quickly followed.

As they stepped out of the bank, the older man took an olive drab canister from his windbreaker, pulled a pin, and tossed it into a distant, empty corner. The canister exploded a few seconds later, immediately filling the bank with a gray-white smoke. The smoke was too thick to allow anyone to make it to the door, so everyone remained on the floor, coughing and crying.

A few minutes later, a couple stepped out of Boojum, the Mexican Burrito Bar. They noticed the smoke in the bank lobby, and the man held the door open, gradually releasing the smoke outside, while his girlfriend called 999, the Irish Emergency Response number. The first Garda vehicle arrived four minutes later.

One

US Marshal Jack Dillon, assigned to Dublin's An Garda Síochána, Special Branch, got the call as he settled onto the couch next to his dog, Lucifer. He had just turned on the 6:00 news, where the leading story was a bank robbery on Hanover Quay, when his phone rang. He checked the screen on his phone, Emergency Response and answered, "Dillon."

"Sir, Emergency Response calling, requesting your presence at 2 Hanover Quay. An AIB bank has been robbed."

It figures, Dillon thought. "Have you contacted DI Suel?"

"Yes, he is en route, sir."

"Mark me as on my way."

"Thank you, sir," the caller said and disconnected. Dillon repeated the address to himself as he entered it into his cellphone's GPS. He turned off the TV, let Lucifer out into the front garden, and hurried up to his bedroom. He strapped on his shoulder holster, pulled a jacket from his closet, and coaxed Lucifer back inside with a biscuit.

He cautiously approached his car, careful not to step in Lucifer's recent deposit, and headed to Hanover Quay. The squad cars, double-parked in front of the AIB bank, identified the location from two blocks away. The building was a seven-story structure. The upper six stories featured all glass housing units with large balconies that were probably going for a million euros each. As he approached, a taxi was just driving away from the South Dock Steak House. Dillon pulled into the spot, took the An Garda Síochána identification sheet from his glove box, and set it on the dashboard. He climbed out of the car, draped the lanyard with his ID around his neck, and headed toward the bank. The building's ground floor units were dark gray concrete with the name of the various businesses, South Dock Steakhouse, AIB Bank, and Boojum, in steel letters above the windows. The bank had a nondescript entrance except for the fact that, right now, the area was taped off by white tape with blue letters that read '**An Garda Síochána**.'

All the lights were on inside the bank, but there was a substance on the windows that limited the view. As he approached, Dillon ran a finger across the exterior of the window but didn't get any residue. Apparently, whatever was on the windows was on the inside. A uniformed officer was standing at the door. As Dillon stepped beneath the An Garda Síochána tape. He held up his ID. The officer nodded and moved aside so Dillon could enter.

At this hour, it was largely An Garda Síochána on the premises. He nodded at a couple of familiar faces and glanced around. He saw three security cameras mounted in different corners. Hopefully, they had been able to record the incident. He headed over to his partner, DI Paddy Suel, who was talking to two individuals at the teller counter.

"Oh, here he is now, finally," Suel said as Dillon approached.

"I literally just got the call not twenty minutes ago. How long have you been here?"

"Five, maybe ten minutes. That's all it took for me to proclaim that a robbery had taken place."

Everyone chuckled. Dillon wrinkled his nose. "I'm guessing they set off a smoke device on the way out. I can smell it, and it's all over the windows."

"And over everything else in here," Suel said and nodded at all the footprints on the floor in what appeared to be very fine dust. "Fortunately, no one was hurt. Two senior individuals were taken to Mater Hospital just to double-check. They were having difficulty breathing after lying in that cloud for ten or fifteen minutes. There's a security tape, not quite four minutes long. We can check it out in the Operations office. It's already been sent to Special Branch. Come on, it's back this way," Suel said and led the way past the teller counter and through a door. There was a short hallway with four doors. They walked past an open office with two officers Dillon recognized. They were speaking with a white-haired man, maybe fifty years old, seated behind a desk.

The nameplate next to the door read Thomas Mullen, President.

The door further down was labeled Operations. Suel knocked on the door as he opened it. Two men were inside. Dillon recognized one of them, Jim Burke, from the Tech Department in the headquarters building. Burke's specialty was facial recognition. They were seated at a desk with three screens mounted on the wall in front of them.

As they stepped in, Burke turned around and said, "Good evening. This is Dermot Casey."

Casey looked up and nodded at Dillon and Suel.

"Dermot has been kind enough to send files to Special Branch and a number of other units. Derm, you want to run that tape for these gentlemen? They're with Special Branch."

Casey nodded but still didn't say anything. His hands flew across the keyboard, and a moment later, three frozen images came up on the screens. One screen focused on the entrance, one focused on the lobby, and the third screen focused on the teller counter. Each image had a twenty-four-hour time in the upper right-hand corner of the screen. At the moment, all three screens displayed the time as 15:54:21. Dillon and Suel stepped behind the two men, and Burke said, "Okay, Derm, play it at normal speed first, then we'll show them the focused version."

Casey ran his fingers across the keyboard, and things began to move on the screen covering the teller counter and the screen covering the lobby. At 15:54:37, the entrance door opened, and two men stepped in. They had long hair that hung over their ears, and they were wearing faded caps, disposable masks, sunglasses, jeans, and what appeared to be navy-blue windbreakers. There were no identifying characteristics on the caps or the windbreakers. One man headed for the teller counter and stood in line behind an older woman. The other man stepped to the counter in the center of the lobby.

As the woman in front of the man stepped aside, he moved forward and handed a note to the teller along with a brown paper bag. They watched as the teller said something, and the man pulled his windbreaker back, exposing the pistol tucked into his belt. As this was going on, the man standing at the counter in the middle of the lobby appeared to be focused on something or someone out of camera range.

The man at the teller counter suddenly moved in front of the woman in the line next to him and said something to the teller. The woman he moved in front of did not appear to be happy and said something to him. Suddenly, the man at the lobby table drew his pistol, fired a shot over his head, and shouted something.

The shot apparently got the attention of everyone, and they began to stretch out on the floor. The teller quickly filled the shopping bag with cash from her drawer. Both tellers disappeared from the screen as they crouched down below the counter. Three individuals could be seen on the lobby screen. All three were lying face down on the floor. One of them, a gray-haired woman, had her hands placed on either side of her head. Both robbers appeared on the lobby screen for a brief moment and then at the door. The man with the shopping bag stepped out of the bank while the other man paused at the door. He took a canister from his windbreaker, pulled a pin, and tossed it into a corner behind him. A moment later, all three screens fogged up. The time in the upper right corners of the screens read 15:58:43. The entire episode took just a few seconds over four minutes.

"There you have it, lads. A few seconds longer than four minutes, probably due to your wan telling your man to mind his manners. They're in and out and disappear."

"What's with the smoke bomb? They're almost out of the place, and no one's going to stop them."

"I'd guess just a precaution," Burke said. "Delay any emergency phone calls or someone following. Teams are in the process of gathering CCTV tapes from surrounding businesses. Anything stand out to you two?"

"That smoke bomb your man sets off. It looked like there was an ID number on the thing. I think his hand was covering up some of it, but I could see L83 in white letters on the canister."

"It's a British military training device," Burke glanced over at a sheet of paper on the desk in front of him. "The actual number is L83A1. A smoke bomb for training purposes in the British army."

"They didn't appear to be current members in the Army," Suel said. "You think they came down from the north?"

"Bring up the images of them stepping in the door, if you would, please, Derm."

Casey typed again, and the clocks on all three screens reverted back to 15:54:21. Only the screen focused on the front door began to count the seconds off. Casey froze the image once both men were present on the screen.

"A few things. As we review the tape, you'll notice these are the only two people wearing face masks. Also, I can't prove it, but my sense is at this early stage that both men are wearing wigs beneath those caps. The windbreakers are nondescript, as are the hats, and I would suggest that both have probably been discarded if not destroyed."

Dillon and Suel studied the image on the screen. Casey's comments made sense.

"With the masks, the sunglasses, and the caps, what chance do you have at facial recognition?"

Burke shook his head. "Almost none. I might be able to narrow it down to a few hundred individuals, but there's almost no chance of coming up with a specific person."

"Do you think this was their first dance?" Suel asked.

"It's quite possible, but if it is, they've studied up on what to do and not to do. If I had to guess, I would say they're students looking to get an advanced degree."

"Students?" Suel asked.

"Not someone attending a university. I meant they're learning as they go along. This may well be their first dance but be prepared to see them again."

TWO

They watched the tape at least a half-dozen times and didn't come up with anything new. Dillon and Suel went back out to the lobby. Dillon walked over to the lobby counter and gazed up at the ceiling, studying.

"What are you looking for?" Suel asked.

"On the security tape, your man pulled out his pistol and fired into the ceiling to get everyone's attention, and he yelled at them to get on the floor."

"Yeah, shooting the gun is certainly one way to get folks to pay attention."

"Take a look and tell me when you can see a bullet hole. I certainly can't find one. He was standing just about here," Dillon said, moving to his right about half a foot. "This rack of deposit and withdrawal slips was centered on his chest on the tape. He raised his arm over his head, pointed at the ceiling, and fired, but I don't see a bullet hole."

Suel looked up and stared at the ceiling, searching. "You think he fired a blank?"

"Right now, I'd say that's entirely possible. I can't see where it hit, and it should have been almost straight upward if it was a live round."

Suel studied the ceiling. "I'm not finding anything. So if they're loaded with blanks, and they've gone to a lot of trouble to get a reasonably small amount of cash, what does that mean?"

"I think it means they've got a lot to learn."

"Did we learn anything from the witnesses?"

Suel shrugged. "The woman that your man jumped in front of was positive he had a Dublin accent. He told her he wasn't finished with his transaction. She told him he should wait his turn and then asked him where he learned his manners. I don't know. It's just not adding up."

"And they've no one working security?" Dillon asked.

"Only before holidays, the last two days, and the first two days of any month. Those would naturally seem to be their busiest times. Dermot Casey is the only employee still here, and he was locked in the room with his security cameras during the robbery. There's Mullen, the president, but he's currently being interviewed, and I suspect they'd take an awfully dim view if we stepped in. You want to wait around until they're finished?"

Dillon shook his head. "I'm thinking we head out, maybe grab a pint. Casey sent us the four-minute tape. It would be interesting to check it out. See if, indeed, they were wearing wigs, for starters. I don't know, Paddy.

You think they might have gone online and just gotten information on how to pull off a robbery? There are all sorts of sites that would have that information. Tell you to wear a disguise. I'm guessing that with the cotton gloves they had on, they probably were wearing latex gloves beneath the cotton to eliminate any DNA trace. No mention of a vehicle parked out front."

"There's a parking ramp around the corner, Dillon. How about this? They park in the ramp. Pull off the robbery and remove the wigs, sunglasses, and windbreakers. One of them hides in the back seat, and the other one drives them out of the garage to someplace where they change. Maybe the car is stolen, they set it on fire, drive off in their own cars, and pretty much vanish into thin air."

"Not so far-fetched. Hopefully, we can trace them on CCTV tapes tomorrow. It's just...I don't know...it doesn't seem to be adding up."

"Yeah, I'm with you. You want to check out the parking ramp around the corner?"

"It couldn't hurt," Dillon said.

"I was afraid you'd say that. Come on, let's do it, but you're buying the pints when we're finished."

The parking ramp was a four-story concrete structure. Payments were all made with credit cards, no cash was accepted, Which meant that the operator's office set between the entrance and exit was empty, and the lights were off.

Dillon and Suel split up, with Suel taking the even levels and Dillon the odd ones. The ramp was only a third full. Lots of open parking places and nothing like windbreakers or wigs lying around. Dillon lifted the lids on the trash bins next to the elevators and found exactly what he expected to find, cups, wrappers, newspapers, junk mail, and three different empty half-pints. He also found a black bra, which was not what he had expected. He had taken the elevator up to the fourth level and worked his way down. It barely took a half-hour. Suel was waiting for him at the exit gate.

"Find anything?" Dillon asked.

"Absolutely nothing. You?"

"Nothing unusual other than a black bra, but I figured you already had one, so I left it in the trash bin."

"Probably a good idea. Hell, we don't even know if they parked in here," Suel said.

"Yeah, although this would be the closest place to disappear from sight. Change to another quick disguise, and one of you hides in the back or even inside the boot, and off you go. With that smoke bomb, even if the Garda arrived in a minute or two, they'd be involved in getting people out of that mess, and the robbers would have all the time in the world to casually exit and drive out of town."

Suel nodded and said, "You aware of a car set on fire anywhere?"

"You mean destroying the evidence? No, I haven't seen anything come across on my phone. Of course, once they're out of the immediate area, hell, they could drive up to Meath or down to Wicklow County and destroy the vehicle or just leave it on the street with the keys in the ignition for some idiot to make off with the thing thinking he'd made a big score."

"I think the best thing we could do would be to adjourn to the Autobahn pub, where you can buy me a pint, and we can discuss what our next move is going to be."

"I can't believe you're starting to make sense, Paddy. Let's go."

Three

Dillon glanced around the pub and asked, "What do you think?"

Suel took a deep breath and exhaled. "I still think we're going to see these two again. Unfortunately, I believe Burke was right. They're using this as a learning experience. How much money do you think they got from today's effort? One, maybe two thousand euros? It strikes me as an awfully big risk to take for that small amount. Given the sense of planning they seem to have put into the operation, wouldn't they have realized, at some point, that there was a finite amount of cash?"

A waitress approached, and Dillon raised his hand, signaling for two more Guinness. "If what you say is true, Paddy, and I'm not suggesting you're wrong. But if that is the case, my thought is we'll see them again sooner rather than later. And if that's the deal, where is their next target? A larger bank? A busier bank? It's not rocket science to realize that today's robbery occurred at a small neighborhood bank for a couple thousand euros. Even if they want to move up the ladder, a larger bank isn't going to work because the place will be too big for two individuals to rob. Plus, a larger bank will have security people who would be armed. That's an entirely new problem that they would have to deal with."

Suel nodded. "Yeah, you're right. But I just can't see them continuing at this level, a couple thousand, and if you're caught, you'll be spending six to ten or maybe even twelve years behind bars."

"But these guys, I don't know. Maybe the ultimate target isn't a bank. Maybe it's a business, someone's office, a jeweler, or even some kind of warehouse."

"It will be interesting to see what, if anything, we're able to get on CCTV footage. Maybe if we—"

The waitress suddenly appeared with two pints of Guinness. She set one in front of Suel and the other in front of Dillon. "Fifteen euros," she said.

"My dad told me he'd buy both pints," Suel grinned and nodded at Dillon.

She looked at Dillon, glanced back at Suel for a brief moment, and joked, "No doubt hoping to get his wayward son back on track."

Dillon laughed, pulled out a twenty euro note, and set it on her tray. "Keep the change. Your comment was worth it."

They clinked glasses and both took a hearty sip.

"You're not aware of these two showing up anywhere in the past, are you?" Suel asked.

Dillon shook his head. "No. If I were, I would have mentioned it. I think it will be interesting to see what comes up on CCTV. My guess is we're going to be looking at next to nothing. At no surprise, the note your man passed to the teller was printed off, so there is no handwriting to compare. A total of seven words, short and to the point."

"Looking at the tapes, what do you think they did wrong?" Suel asked and took another sip.

"In all honesty, not much. Were it not for your wan, giving the man a hard time, they may have been able to walk out of there, and no one would have been the wiser. Only firing the pistol, apparently, a blank, is what got everyone's attention and got them on the ground. I find it interesting they didn't collect wallets and purses. It's not unusual to gather all that up."

Suel nodded. "Yeah, but in the instances where it's been done, there's usually a group large enough to have one or two people in charge of that. Just the two of them? It would have put them on the security cameras for another minute, maybe two. The fact that they didn't do that suggests they had at least a rudimentary plan going in. It seems obvious they wanted to get out of there as quickly as possible."

"Yeah, and it seemed to work. I still like the idea of the smoke bomb being used to get the Gardai focused on moving people out of the lobby and not looking for the robbers, or at least giving them time to casually disappear and not attract any attention. Hopefully, we'll get a car and license number on CCTV, and that will be the end of it. I'm still coming back to why in the hell anyone would do this. They've got about a ten percent chance of not getting caught, and for what? Two thousand euros? It's crazy."

"Yeah, that's the bottom line." Suel drained his glass. "Hey, thanks for the pint. I'll catch you in the morning."

They walked out together and headed home. Dillon drove past Tara's house, just across the lane and up a couple of doors from his place. There was a gray Volkswagen Golf parked out front, and the drapes in the sitting room were drawn, meaning she was entertaining someone or being entertained. He pulled into the front garden, let Lucifer out, and made himself a grilled cheese sandwich. Once he finished eating, he let Lucifer back in. He scanned the TV for a movie, but nothing caught his interest. He watched the tail end of the late evening news and headed up to bed.

Four

Since it was Saturday morning, Dillon woke up forty-five minutes before his alarm would normally go off. He hadn't set the alarm, so, of course, he didn't sleep in. He crawled out of bed, pulled on a sweat suit, and headed downstairs. He put the coffee on and turned on his laptop. He had eleven emails waiting, not one of any interest. He didn't need a new mattress, he was happy with his car and home insurance, and then there were the three political emails from people he would never vote for. He deleted one after another and cleared his emails in about ten seconds. He logged into YouTube, brought up last night's US evening news, and listened to that while he prepared his breakfast.

Halfway through breakfast, Lucifer appeared, and Dillon let him out into the front garden. He finished breakfast, filled Lucifer's food and water dishes, and let him back inside. He checked the local Dublin news, nothing really of interest and only a brief mention of the AIB robbery yesterday afternoon. He went upstairs, shaved, grabbed a shower, and hopped in the car. As he backed out of his drive, it wasn't lost on him that whoever belonged to the gray Volkswagen Golf at Tara's house across the lane was still there this morning. He drove to his office in the An Garda Síochána Headquarters building located alongside Phoenix Park.

He parked close to the main door and entered the building. Once in the Special Branch section, he settled in at his desk and opened the first of a half-dozen files regarding yesterday's AIB robbery. He examined the images of the two individuals as they entered the bank. He focused on the faces, enlarging the images and examining the little he could see of the hairlines on the two individuals. Burke had suggested that both men were wearing long-haired wigs beneath their caps, and Dillon was inclined to agree.

The two men had on disposable masks, but Dillon noted that the suspect with the blonde hair had what appeared to be maybe a half-day's beard growth in the area of his sideburn and hairs in his ear that appeared brown or possibly auburn. If he'd shaved first thing in the morning, the beard growth Dillon was studying would make sense at almost four in the afternoon.

The sunglasses on both men were reflective, and for a half moment, Dillon recalled snapshots of his father as a young man in a US Army uniform wearing mirrored sunglasses upon his arrival home from Viet Nam.

He studied the wrists on both individuals looking for a hint of latex gloves underneath the brown cotton work gloves. The gloves were tucked into the elastic-reinforced sleeves of the nylon windbreakers, and he was unable to detect any latex. Examining other images, he noted the remnants from labels that had been cut off from the rear of both pairs of blue jeans.

He couldn't be sure, but the pistol that the one suspect held and fired appeared to have a black carbon fiber finish. He enlarged the image, but it blurred what he thought might be the manufacturer's name to the point that he couldn't make it out.

He made a list of questions and suggestions regarding the wigs, actual hair color, and the type of weapon and sent them to Emily down in the Tech Lab. That done, he headed out of the office, made a quick stop at his local Aldi grocery store, and drove home. This time, the Volkswagen Golf was gone from Tara's house.

Lucifer met him at the door and hurried out into the front garden. Dillon put the groceries away, grabbed the leash, and took Lucifer on a walk. They did three laps around Albert Park just outside of DCU, Dublin City University. Each lap was 1.2 miles, and when they'd finished the third lap, both Dillon and Lucifer were ready to head home.

Dillon placed a call to Aiofe McDonald, a woman he'd dated off and on, and ended up leaving a message. "Hi Aiofe, Jack Dillon calling. It's been too long since we went out. Just wondering if you'd like to join me for dinner this evening. Nowhere in particular, but I'm in the mood to eat in a restaurant for a change. Just let me know, and I'll gladly pick you up."

He disconnected, then went upstairs, changed the sheets on his bed, vacuumed the bedroom, and cleaned the bathroom sink and the glass in the shower. He had dozed off on the couch in front of the TV when his phone rang. He cleared his throat and answered in what he hoped was a sexy voice, "Jack Dillon."

"Are you okay, Dillon? You sound like shite," Suel said.

"Oh, you, I was hoping it was a woman I'd called and left a message asking her to dinner."

"Oh, for lord's sake, forget it. If she has any brains, she won't be calling the likes of you back. Hey, listen. I'm going to be watching the rugby match on the telly tonight. We're playing the All Blacks, New Zealand's team. If you're not too busy, why don't you pick up some beer and come over."

"Yeah, I suppose I can do that. If I don't hear from that woman in the next thirty minutes, I'll give you a call and—"

"Dillon, it's almost 5:00. You're not going to hear from her. Come on over. Oh, and don't forget the beer," Suel said and disconnected.

Dillon walked into the kitchen. Suel was right. It was almost 5:00. He'd apparently been asleep for an hour and a half. Aiofe hadn't returned his call, and whether he liked it or not, he knew he probably wouldn't hear from her. He let Lucifer out into the front garden, then went upstairs, showered, and changed. On the way to Suel's, he stopped at a local shop and grabbed a twelve-pack of Smithwick's Blonde Ale. He parked in front of Suel's place ten minutes later.

Given Suel's character, you'd expect a place with overgrown grass, gardens filled with weeds, and maybe two or three newspapers on the front steps. Just the opposite was the case. The lawn was always neatly trimmed, and the gardens, edged with stones painted white, had a number of different flowers, not to mention a half-dozen rose bushes and two rose trees. The two front windows had flower boxes with a lovely array of red and yellow flowers.

Dillon stepped into the front garden. Just as he closed the gate behind him, Suel opened the front door wearing jeans, a long sleeve Irish rugby jersey, dark green with a white collar, and a black apron. "Aww, Paddy, how nice of you to get all dressed up for me."

Suel shook his head, took the twelve-pack of beer from Dillon, and said, "Believe me, I didn't dress up for the likes of you. Come on in. You're the first one here."

Dillon stepped inside and followed Suel into the kitchen. He could see three roast chickens through the window on the oven door. "The first one here? You've got other folks coming?"

"Not to worry, the two of us plus my friend Sean and three others."

"Three others? You should have told me. I would have picked up a case of beer instead of just the twelve-pack."

"We've plenty of beer and wine, and if things get desperate, I have a half-dozen whiskeys. Here make yourself useful and toss this," Suel said as he slid a wooden salad bowl across the counter to Dillon. A salad fork and spoon were already in the bowl.

Dillon began tossing the salad as Suel opened a bag of green beans and dumped them into a frying pan. A moment later, the doorbell rang.

"Oh, that should be Sean. Would you mind letting him in?"

"I'm on it," Dillon said as he hopped off the stool and stepped into the entryway. He opened the door and was about to say, 'Hi, Sean,' until he focused on the red-haired woman holding what looked like a white bakery box.

She was maybe six inches shorter than Dillon. Dressed in tight white shorts, with a black belt and a red and white striped off-the-shoulder top. She smiled and said, "Oh dear. I hope I'm in the right place. Does Paddy Suel live here?"

"He does, and he's cooking in the kitchen at the moment. I work with him. My name is Jack Dillon," he said as he held out his hand.

"Noreen Rooney, nice to meet you," she said as they shook hands.

"Let me take this for you," Dillon said and took hold of the bakery box.

"Dessert," she said. "Thank you. So you work with Paddy? Are you the American he's always talking about?"

"Probably, but don't believe whatever he said. I'm really a very nice guy."

She laughed as Dillon closed the door behind her. "He only says nice things about you."

"Then he's one of the few," Dillon said, and she laughed again as they headed into the kitchen.

"Oh, Noreen, thanks for coming. The other girls should be here shortly. Can I get you a beer or a glass of wine?"

"A glass of wine would be wonderful. White, if you have it."

"Coming right up. You met my partner, Dillon? Hopefully, he didn't say anything too rude or insulting."

"No, he was very polite. Oh, I baked all day and made a dessert, then placed it in that box."

"How very thoughtful," Suel said as he filled a wine glass and handed it across the counter to her.

"Thoughtful? You told me I had to bring it, or you weren't going to let me in."

The doorbell rang, and Suel said, "There's trouble. You mind letting them in, Noreen?"

She took a sip of her wine, set the glass on the counter, and said, "Watch this for me, and don't let Paddy drink any, please." The doorbell rang again as she stepped into the entry.

They heard the door open, and then a male voice said, "Oh, Noreen, here to keep us all in line?"

"Come on. We're all in the kitchen. How you keeping, Sean?"

"Good, thanks for asking. Not a bother."

Everyone chatted, sipped their drinks, and Suel eventually took the chickens out of the oven. "We shouldn't wait any longer for the Mahoney sisters. They'll simply have to catch up," Suel said just as the doorbell rang.

Noreen hurried out of the kitchen, and a moment later, the three men heard shrieks and laughter. "Oh God, prepare yourselves, gentlemen. With the three of them we'll be lucky to get a word in."

To be continued . . .

Thanks for taking the time to check out the Jack Dillon Dublin tale, <u>Retirement Scheme</u>. Things are about to get very interesting and a lot more complicated. Better grab your copy. Enjoy the read!

Books by Mike Faricy
Crime Fiction Firsts

A boxset of the first four books in four crime fiction series:

Russian Roulette; Dev Haskell series
Welcome; Jack Dillon Dublin Tales series
Corridor Man; Corridor Man series
Reduced Ransom! Hot Shot series

The following titles comprise the Dev Haskell series:

Russian Roulette: Case 1
Mr. Swirlee: Case 2
Bite Me: Case 3
Bombshell: Case 4
Tutti Frutti: Case 5
Last Shot: Case 6
Ting-A-Ling: Case 7
Crickett: Case 8
Bulldog: Case 9
Double Trouble: Case 10
Yellow Ribbon: Case 11
Dog Gone: Case 12
Scam Man: Case 13
Foiled: Case 14
What Happens in Vegas… Case 15
Art Hound: Case 16
The Office: Case 17

Star Struck: Case 18
International Incident: Case 19
Guest From Hell: Case 20
Art Attack: Case 21
Mystery Man: Case 22
Bow-Wow Rescue: Case 23
Cold Case: Case 24
Cash Up Front: Case 25
Dream House: Case 26
Alley Katz: Case 27
The Big Gamble: Case 28
Bad to the Bone: Case 29
Silencio!: Case 30
Surprise, Surprise: Case 31
Hit & Run: Case 32
Suspect Santa: Case 33
P.I. Apprentice: Case 34
Rebel Without a Clue: Case 35
Puppy Love: Case 36

The following titles are Dev Haskell novellas:
Dollhouse
The Dance
Pixie
Fore!
Twinkle Toes
(*a Dev Haskell short story*)

The following are Dev Haskell Boxsets:
Dev Haskell Boxset 1-3
Dev Haskell Boxset 4-6
Dev Haskell Boxset 7-9
Dev Haskell Boxset 10-12
Dev Haskell Boxset 13-15
Dev Haskell Boxset 16-18
Dev Haskell Boxset 19-21
Dev Haskell Boxset 22-24
Dev Haskell Boxset 25-27
Dev Haskell Boxset 28-30
Dev Haskell Boxset 1-7
Dev Haskell Boxset 8-14
Dev Haskell Boxset 15-19
Dev Haskell Boxset 20-24
Dev Haskell Boxset 25-29

The following titles comprise the Jack Dillon Dublin Tales series:
Welcome
Jack Dillon Dublin Tale 1
Sweet Dreams
Jack Dillon Dublin Tale 2
Mirror Mirror
Jack Dillon Dublin Tale 3
Silver Bullet
Jack Dillon Dublin Tale 4
Fair City Blues

Jack Dillon Dublin Tale 5
Spade Work
Jack Dillon Dublin Tale 6
Madeline Missing
Jack Dillon Dublin Tale 7
Mistaken Identity
Jack Dillon Dublin Tale 8
Picture Perfect
Jack Dillon Dublin Tale 9
Dublin Moon
Jack Dillon Dublin Tale 10
Mystery Woman
Jack Dillon Dublin Tale 11
Second Chance
Jack Dillon Dublin Tale 12
Payback Brother
Jack Dillon Dublin Tale 13
The Heist
Jack Dillon Dublin Tale 14
Jewels To Kill For
Jack Dillon Dublin Tale 15
Retirement Scheme
Jack Dillon Dublin Tale 16
The Collector
Jack Dillon Dublin Tale 17

Jack Dillon Dublin Tales Boxsets:
Jack Dillon Dublin Tales 1-3
Jack Dillon Dublin Tales 4-6

Jack Dillon Dublin Tales 1-5
Jack Dillon Dublin Tales 1-7
Jack Dillon Dublin Tales 6-10

The following titles comprise the Hotshot series;
Reduced Ransom! Second Edition
Finders Keepers! Second Edition
Bankers Hours Second Edition
Chow Down Second Edition
Moonlight Dance Academy Second Edition
Irish Dukes (Fight Card Series)
written under the pseudonym Jack Tunney

The following titles comprise the Corridor Man series:
Corridor Man
Corridor Man 2: Opportunity knocks
Corridor Man 3: The Dungeon
Corridor Man 4: Dead End
Corridor Man 5: Finger
Corridor Man 6: Exit Strategy
Corridor Man 7: Trunk Music
Corridor Man 8: Birthday Boy
Corridor Man 9: Boss Man
Corridor Man 10: Bye Bye Bobby

Corridor Man novellas:
Corridor Man: Valentine
Corridor Man: Auditor

Corridor Man: Howling
Corridor Man: Spa Day

The following are Corridor Man Boxsets:
Corridor Man Boxset 1-3
Corridor Man Boxset 1-5
Corridor Man Boxset 6-9

All books are available on Amazon.com

Thank you!

Contact the author:
- Email: mikefaricyauthor@gmail.com
- Twitter: @Mikefaricybooks
- Facebook: Mike Faricy Author
- Website: http://www.mikefaricybooks.com

Published by

MJF Publishing

www.ingramcontent.com/pod-product-compliance
Lightning Source LLC
Chambersburg PA
CBHW070521310726
48976CB00002BA/503